ADVANCE PRAISE FOR

The Bachelorette Party

"The writing is SUPERB! The biggest laugh and cry I have had in a long time."   —FREDA PAYNE, singer

"Don's writing brings to life the diversity of women's issues with honesty and emotion."

—KENNY LATTIMORE, singer

"*The Bachelorette Party* has me convinced that Don Welch bugged the ladies' room and has been listening to all our dirt for years."   —ANNA MARIA HORSFORD, actress

"*The Bachelorette Party* is a wild ride on the secret side of what we ladies laugh about, cry about, try to hide from our friends . . . and even at times ourselves! The stage play is a must-see . . . this book, a must-read!"

—DAWNN LEWIS, actress, singer, composer, producer

"Don writes as if he were a fly on the wall in a group therapy session."   —FRED THOMAS JR., director, filmmaker

The Bachelorette Party

The
Bachelorette
Party

a novel

Donald Welch

ONE WORLD

BALLANTINE BOOKS • NEW YORK

A One World Books Trade Paperback Original

Copyright © 2008 by Donald Welch
All rights reserved.

Published in the United States by One World Books,
an imprint of The Random House Publishing Group,
a division of Random House, Inc., New York.

ONE WORLD is a registered trademark and the One World
colophon is a trademark of Random House, Inc.

Library of Congress Cataloging-in-Publication Data
Welch, Donald.
The bachelorette party: a novel / Donald Welch.
p. cm.
ISBN 978-0-345-50161-5 (pbk.)
1. Young women—Fiction.   2. Friendship—Fiction.   3. Weddings—
Fiction.   4. Parties—Fiction.   I. Title.
PS3623.E463B33   2008
813'.6—dc22   2008005077

Printed in the United States of America

www.oneworldbooks.net

2   4   6   8   9   7   5   3   1

Book design by Nancy Beth Field

To my mother, Gloria Welch Pollitt,
and in memory of my grandmother
Mary Welch ("Momma").
I am the man I am because of
your unconditional love.

Author's Note

Dear Readers:

As a man I don't profess to have some deep insight into the female psyche, but I've been told that I have an innate ability to listen, really listen, to what women have to say—something a lot of my "brothahs" don't do. The women you will read about in this novel are no strangers to me. I know them and am convinced you do too. They are our sisters, friends, lovers, and family.

The Bachelorette Party is based on my hit stage play of the same name. After performances, women would come up to me and tell me that they saw themselves or knew people who represented the characters in my play. Word of mouth caused news of the play to spread like wildfire and more than seventy-five performances later, I'm pleased to share with you my first novel.

Writing my first novel was both a wonderful and pain-staking process. It gave me an opportunity to expand upon characters who became so dear to my heart. While the play took place on one night, Nicole's bachelorette party, with the novel I was able to show these women's backgrounds and give you a glimpse into their childhood, teenage years, and up through their present, including the aftermath of the bachlorette party. I was able to inject more humor, more drama, and even more sisterhood into a story that I hope will linger with your spirit long after you finish reading the last page.

I began writing this novel in the middle of two national tours of my stage plays, all the while heading up my production company, Don B. Welch Productions, and through this process, I've found that writing can sometimes be a lonely craft, separating the writer from family, friends, and lovers, sometimes for days and weeks on end. But I am smart enough to know that without all of the above, this book would not be possible. For this I am both thankful and grateful.

My profound love and respect for women, especially black women, is unquestionable. Their beauty, strength, and undying love has cradled me from infancy to adulthood. My mother and grandmother not only showered my brother, Vernon, and me with unconditional love, but also everyone else they knew. My grandmother—"Momma" as we all called her—was a 5'2" black woman from the South who migrated to the Philadelphia area in the 1940's, with two children and no more than a third-grade education. Despite her lack of formal education, she was one of the smartest and most self-sufficient women I've ever known.

Many times throughout my childhood, college years, and adulthood I would seek my grandmother's and my mom's advice on life and love, and before making tough decisions. When you are constantly told that you can be anything or go anywhere in this world without fear as long as you have the love of God in your heart—well that is some powerful stuff. "Momma" is gone now, but on occasion I find myself still talking to her and seeking advice. I'm blessed to still have my mother and we are best friends.

With so many negative stereotypical images of black women constantly being displayed on screen, stage, and in books, I hope that *The Bachelorette Party* is a welcome change. Sure it's peppered with adult language and situations, and the ladies might display "home girl" attitudes at times, but look closely, and you'll see a group of smart, intelligent, beautiful, loyal, and sexy black women—all different, but in the end, all the same. They live hard, love hard, laugh hard, play hard, and cry hard. But through it all, their strength prevails.

So there you have it, my friends. This is the first of what I hope are many novels to come. My baby: *The Bachelorette Party*. And remember: The day you stop dreaming you might as well stop breathing.

Living my life like it's golden,
Donald Welch

The Bachelorette Party

PROLOGUE

Daydreaming

STANDING IN HER wedding dress, Nicole Lawson caught her reflection in the glass doors of the church, and for the very first time in her life she truly knew what beautiful felt like. *Everything* about the day was beautiful. *Yes,* she thought, *including me*. She started to cry.

"You all right, baby girl?" her father's soothing voice whispered in her ear.

Nicole was too overcome with emotion to respond.

"Baby, you ready?"

"Huh? Oh, sorry, Daddy. Yes, of course I'm ready."

Was she ever.

As she walked down the aisle, she couldn't help but admire her sisterfriends lined up so pretty and regal, smiling at her through her veil. They had been through so much

together. Most groups of friends like them hung for a
while, and then through the years a few dropped off here
and there. But not them: Freda, Denise, Valerie, Keisha,
Zenora, Renee, Mira, and Tisha—all her girls.

Wait! Why was Keisha holding her goddaughter
Kimmy? Of course, Tisha was late again. *Damn, Tish, even
on my wedding day?* Nicole thought. Tisha Grant was
chronically late for everything. *Now I'm pissed. She
promised me that today, of all days, she'd be on time.*

Music interrupted Nicole's brief flash of anger. Miss
Landis, the church musical director, played the organ
music as Freda made her way to the microphone.

Freda began to sing "All In Love Is Fair," and her voice
was in rare form. *Sing it!*

Nicole's legs turned to rubber. "Daddy, hold me up,
okay?"

"I got you, baby girl," he whispered. He then chuckled
and said, "No time to get cold feet now. Alan is waiting for
you."

Despite her anxiety, Nicole noticed the wonderful job
her mother and the wedding coordinator had done. Gladioli and lilies, her favorite flowers, filled the church with
their scent. Candles were arranged at the altar in a half-
moon pattern adding to the tranquil mood. Nicole and her
mother had pored over every bride and wedding publication on the magazine stands for suggestions on selecting
the "perfect" gown and decorations. The entire sanctuary
went beyond Nicole's expectations, and she wanted to
keep a picture of it in her memory forever.

Something drew Nicole's attention to the leftmost back pews. She was surprised to see Tisha sitting completely alone. Through her veil, Nicole attempted to signal Tisha to join the other bridesmaids before she made her march down the aisle, but Tisha didn't budge.

I'll deal with her lateness at another time. But not now. Not on my beautiful day.

With tears in her eyes and an angelic smile, Tisha looked her way and mouthed the words, *I love you.*

If Tisha could have seen Nicole's expression under the veil, she'd know that Nicole was rolling her eyes.

Nicole and her father began their slow march, and all eyes turned their way. Nicole could feel her father's pride as she leaned on his arm.

She noticed that Mrs. Ward, the mother of her childhood friend Adrienne, had come. It had been years since Nicole had last seen Mrs. Ward, whose hair was now white as cotton. Thoughts of Adrienne came to her. They'd promised to be in each other's weddings, but that wasn't to be. Nicole still missed her childhood friend and hoped that Adrienne was looking down on her from above. A familiar-looking young girl sat with Mrs. Ward. Perhaps it was her niece, who looked about twelve or thirteen, the same age as Adrienne when she passed away.

Yes, everything looked absolutely beautiful. It was the happiest day of Nicole's life. She was even willing to forgive Tisha for being late. *At least she's here. Thank goodness Roland, that bastard of a husband of hers, didn't come.* Nicole was surprised that Roland even let Tisha go anywhere without him. How she ended up with him, Nicole could never figure out. Once she believed Tisha was the most cautious out of all the girls as far as men. Tisha had a good track record for choosing decent brothas, but that all changed when she met Roland. None of them liked him very much, but Nicole tolerated him because he was her girl's man, and her goddaughter's father. Otherwise, Nicole had little use for Roland, and he didn't hesitate to return the sentiment.

Okay, enough of that, Nicole Lawson; it's your day.

Alan patiently stood at the altar next to his best man and cousin, Pete, who looked as nervous as she felt.

This is it! The day I've waited for all my life.

Nicole and her father reached the pulpit. He kissed her lightly on the cheek, whispered he loved her, and joined her mother in the front row.

Alan took Nicole's hand, and they turned toward Reverend Roberts. He smiled, opened his hymnal, and began to announce their vows.

Ring! Ring!

Nicole couldn't believe it. Someone's cell phone was going off. She immediately assumed it was Keisha because she never went anywhere without her cell phone. Nicole cut an angry stare her way, and Keisha threw back one of her own hard looks that read, *Bitch, it's not mine. So there!*

RING!

This time it was even louder. Nicole decided that she would personally kill the owner of that damn phone.

Ring!

No one was scurrying to turn off the cell.

Ring!

"Will somebody answer *that*!" Nicole shouted.

Hello, who is this? Who?

"It's Rocky, Miss Girl. Where are you at, diva?"

One

I Can See Clearly Now

NICOLE WOKE from her dream, her *beautiful* dream. Rocky was calling from Zenora's salon. *Oh, shit. I overslept,* she thought. *What time is it?*

"It's ten fifteen, Nicole. Your appointment was—"

Nicole cut Rocky off before he finished, "Ten o'clock. I know. Tell Z I'll be there in twenty. Okay, gotta go."

In three moves, Nicole hung up, sprang out of bed, and jumped in the shower. Her head was killing her. *What the hell was that dream about? Jesus! Nerves must have gotten the best of me before my wedding day tomorrow,* Nicole thought to herself. *Is that alarm clock working?* As the hot water cascaded down her face and body, she glanced at her feet. "Oh, shit!" she yelled. She forgot to add a pedicure to today's appointment.

She ran into her large walk-in closet, which housed

more than 250 pairs of shoes and enough clothes (some with tags still on them) to open a small boutique. Nicole's shoes were arranged neatly on wooden racks, and her clothes were hung according to season and color. She quickly grabbed her favorite Gap jeans and paired it with a Roberto Cavalli jacket. She may be late, but she was going to be fierce.

○ ○ ○

THE DRIVE TO ZENORA'S was quick, and all the traffic lights worked in Nicole's favor. Nicole couldn't stop analyzing that dream. *Why was Tisha late for the ceremony and sitting in the corner of the church? Why was Keisha holding Kimmy?* Her mind searched for some type of explanation.

Nicole had almost reached the shop when her cell rang, but she didn't answer it, because she figured it was probably Zenora ready to curse her out for being late and for not taking her suggestion to make the appointment on Thursday. Going to a black salon on Friday or Saturday, no matter how early you got there, usually turned into an all-day affair.

Luckily, Nicole found a parking space right in front of the shop. She prepared herself to apologize to Z for her lateness and plead with her for a pedicure on the busiest day at the salon, hoping Z would be sympathetic.

Nicole rushed through the front door and was greeted by Marcella, Zenora's receptionist, who was seated behind a fuchsia-and-white counter that reflected the décor of the salon. Activity was bustling at every station. Marcella smiled and said, "Hello, Nicole." Nicole returned the greeting as Marcella checked her in by first bringing up her data on the salon's computer database, including operator, treatment, and appointment. She then handed Nicole a fuchsia-colored smock and escorted her to a changing area.

Nicole looked around, proud of all her girl had accomplished. Everything Zenora touched turned to gold, and this salon was evidence of that. Women were pampered at Zenora's like you wouldn't believe. Z's staff of fourteen attended to their clients' every need. Weaves, braids, more weaves, shampoos, more weaves, color and tint jobs, perms, manicures, facials, and more weaves!

There were eight stations and a luxurious waiting area near the receptionist's desk. Each station was adorned with professional artwork. Hardwood floors gave the salon a showroom flourish.

Those scheduled for facials and waxings were escorted to a private room for service. Behind the desk display cases offered top-of-the-line beauty products, from mink eyelashes to luxury foot cream to a new line that Z imported from Italy, which was bringing in even more clients just for the products. Nicole blushed as she thought of the imported lemon bath gel—it drove Alan wild when they showered together with it.

There was only one thing Z didn't tolerate, and that was lateness. If a client was more than ten minutes late for an appointment, she might as well forget it and reschedule her appointment for a future date, because each stylist was instructed to move on to the next client. No excuses. No exceptions.

The last time Nicole was in, a mother had arrived late with her seventeen-year-old daughter, who needed a hairdo for that evening's prom. Her appointment with Rocky was scheduled for 9:15 a.m. They arrived at 9:26 a.m. The teenager wanted microbraids, which could take as long as eight to nine hours to complete. Noticing the client had not arrived at 9:25 a.m., Rocky shouted, "Any walk-ins? Next!" Just like that, the chair was occupied. A minute later, the door swung open and the two ladies came rushing in. When the women saw somebody else in Rocky's chair, the mother screamed like somebody had just died. You'd think that all the activity in the shop would come to a complete halt. Not at Zenora's. Everyone continued whatever they were doing, knowing full well it was merely some poor soul late for her appointment.

Feeling bad for the teenager, Nicole went over to Rocky to make a plea.

"Rocky, it's her prom. C'mon, look at her. She's all upset. It's a once-in-a-lifetime event for a young woman. She's crying."

Without even a slight glance at either mother or daughter, Rocky said, "I guess so. It's cryin' time! Miss Thing knows that we don't play that shit in here. I spoke with her yesterday when she stopped by to confirm and reminded her about her appointment and our policy. I told her it would probably be in her best interest to arrive fifteen minutes earlier than her scheduled time. She played it off, waving me down with her hand and rolling her eyes, saying 'Chile, don't worry, we'll be here.' So I don't want to hear that crap!"

Defeated, the mother started to attack Rocky, who continued chewing his gum and prepping his next client. She spoke loud enough for Rocky and everyone in the reception area to hear: "We only came here in the first place because he was our last resort. He's not that good at braiding damn hair anyway." As she made her exit, she sneered, "Faggot!"

Time stood still: Everything and everyone in the shop came to a complete halt. It even seemed like the Whitney Houston song on the CD player stopped midway.

Rocky excused himself from his client and calmly walked over to the pair. He leaned toward the mother with a hard stare and then whispered something in her ear. When he finished, the woman looked at him with a terrified expression and, without saying a word, shot out the door like a cannon. Rocky smoothed the bottom of his smock and, with the grace of a ballerina, floated back over to his station. The intrusion was over and everything resumed like clockwork: conversations, the sound of hair dryers, running water, even Miss Whitney finished her new song.

Nicole later asked Z what Rocky had said to the woman.

Z laughed and said, "He told her 'Bitch, I will run this flat iron so far up your ass that the cherry you *thought* you lost seventeen years ago when you *had* that ugly-ass daughter of yours will fly out yo' nose like a red boogie! And furthermore, *Mommy,* try asking your husband how well I braid hair, because when I was on his back and he was facedown in my pillow whimpering like a newborn kitten, I noticed how *masterful my* skills *were!*"

Whew! Rocky didn't waste words.

○ ° ○

BUT TODAY IT WAS Nicole who was late. *I might as well get it over with,* Nicole thought. *No lies, just go in, tell her what happened, and pray that this one time she will forgive me and let me in the chair.* Nicole didn't take for granted the fact that Z had been her girl since high school, because sister girl had made it very clear on past occasions that she didn't mix business and friends. Friend or no friend, there were two things you didn't fuck with when it came to Zenora: her business and her men. She'd say, "Black people need to be retrained. How many times have we sat at a concert or movie theater and it does not start on time, or if it does, some of our 'cousins' will sashay in fifteen or twenty minutes late and be loud about it?"

Nicole hoped she could catch a break because Z was on the phone, and her chair was still empty. Z approached her station without saying a word and motioned with her hand for Nicole to sit in the chair, all the while rolling her eyes. Nicole chuckled to herself, got seated, and prepared to receive the dressing down she had coming to her. She could tell by the tone of Zenora's conversation that she was talking to one of her many *chulos.*

"*Papi*, I can't," she said in a low tone. "You know I'm at work. And tonight's my girl's bachelorette party."

Whatever he said next made her giggle like a teenager, because she sighed heavily after hanging up, shook her head, and said, "Lord have mercy."

Nicole waited for her tongue-lashing, but to her surprise, Zenora said nothing, so she decided to speak first.

"Zenora girl, I know I'm late. I'm sorry."

Zenora didn't respond, and after the pause that followed, Nicole continued.

"I overslept. That's never happened to me. I had a terrible, restless night with the craziest shit in my head and the weirdest dream. If Rocky hadn't called me, I'd still be asleep. Obviously, I was more tired than I thought. I actually went to bed early last night. I know it's no excuse, but it's the truth."

Silence.

"Z, I'm sorry. Damn!"

"Girl, I haven't said anything to you, so why are you trippin'? You're in the chair, aren't you?"

"Yes, but you're giving me the silent treatment."

"Please, I got my mind on Ernesto. I'm not thinking about you." She smiled.

"You had your eye on him for two weeks now. Isn't he working on the building across the street?"

"Yes. We've been playing cat and mouse with each other ever since. In fact, our first official date was the other night, and girl, let me tell you, my 'space heater' hasn't been the same since!"

"You are so crazy."

"He wants to hook up tonight, but I told him about the party and that there was no way I could slip out now, because my girl, who was running late for her hair appointment, is in the chair now. And because we've been friends for years and she's getting married tomorrow, I'm going to let her slide this one time."

"Okay, okay, I knew you'd get it all out. You have *officially read* me, but thanks, girl, I really appreciate it. And, oh, could I ask one more favor? Could you squeeze me in for a pedicure, too?"

"Girl, you are pushing your luck. Be glad you're getting married tomorrow. Otherwise I'd make you reschedule."

Raising an eyebrow while running her fingers through Nicole's hair, Zenora teased, "I thought maybe Alan came through last night and 'touched you up,' and you just couldn't get it together this morning."

"I wish. No we both decided that we would stop seeing each other at least two days before our wedding because there's so much to do on both our ends. We'll do all of our catching up on our wedding night. Besides, his parents are staying over at his place, and he knew Valerie was going to be at my spot when she got in town for the wedding."

"Oh, that's right. I forgot about that. How is she? It's been a couple of weeks since we spoke."

"She's fine. She's arriving today after meeting up with her Realtor."

"How's that comin' along? The last time we spoke, she was closing the deal on the building. I'm really happy for

Val. That girl has always wanted to open her own business."

"True." I added, "She has always admired you and Keisha for owning and operating your businesses."

At that moment, Marcella interrupted their private girl talk. "Zenora, Vanessa Bell Calloway is on the phone. She wants to know if it's possible to fit her in around five p.m. today? She just got word from her agent that they will need her on the set tomorrow."

"All right, Mo, tell her five o'clock it is, but to leave her cell phone in the hotel room 'cause she's on the phone more than the operator."

Marcella laughed and then returned to the front desk phone to confirm the appointment with Miss Calloway.

"Vanessa Bell Calloway, huh? I didn't even know you knew her, Zenora."

"I don't. Not really, anyway. Star Jones Reynolds turned her on to me. She's one of her best friends and is now in Philly filming the new M. Night Shyamalan movie. You know all his films are done here."

"Vanessa should be working more," I said. "She's so underrated."

"You could say that about so many others," Zenora remarked, "like Angela Bassett and Lynn Whitfield, two gorgeous, talented actresses that Hollywood rarely uses. When Angela got the Oscar nomination for *What's Love Got to Do with It,* everyone assumed it would open up so many doors for her. Same thing with Lynn's Emmy win for *The Josephine Baker Story,* but the offers didn't come.

Keisha and I had this conversation last week while she was getting her hair done. As always, you know she came in here armed with some rag magazine in tow. There was an article called 'The Hollywood Blackout: Where Are Our Black Actresses?' I mentioned that if Angela and Lynn were white, not only would they be gracing the covers of *People* or *US Weekly* magazines regularly, but they would have tons of film and TV offers to choose from. Now being forty-plus women, they're routinely reduced to secondary parts and nonleading roles. Even the black filmmakers are only hiring them as aunts, mothers, and neighbors, when in fact, not only are these women talented, but they're beautiful and sexy as well. Now Goldie Hawn, Sharon Stone, and Susan Sarandon work all the time and are offered sexy leading roles. Hell, Diane Keaton was practically nude in the film *Something's Gotta Give*."

Zenora was on a roll. "Keisha got invited to an Oscar-viewing party the year Halle Berry won for Best Actress. During Halle's speech, she spoke about Hollywood embracing her and accepting her into the community and how she was so happy. Hell, we were all happy for her! But crazy-ass Keisha was like, 'Bitch please, let's see how many major films you get after tonight when yo' ass can command the same paycheck as them heffas like Cameron Diaz, Jodie Foster, or Gwyneth Paltrow.' "

"Hmmm, Keisha's right," Nicole said. "Halle *does* work, but not like they do."

The salon's front door opened and closed like an automatic revolving door, causing Nicole to remark, "Z, if this keeps up, you're going to have to open a third shop to accommodate your clientele."

Zenora just smiled. "Girl, if I have my way, my plan for this time next year is to just sit back and let the business run itself."

"Really?"

"Yeah, girl. I'm getting tired. I've been doing hair since I was fourteen, working part-time in my aunt's makeshift salon that she ran from her house in North Philly. I'm thirty-two, and as young as that may be, there's a whole lot more of this great big world I'd like to see and experience. Getting time off for something like that is difficult in my business."

"Well, that's what you get for being so good at what you do. What will your personal clients do? There are a lot of sistahs that will not let anyone touch their heads but Zenora Blakey. It's your fault that you have us all spoiled."

"As flattered as I am, baby, you're right. But there's got to be more for my life than doing hair. And it's funny you mentioned a third shop, because I'm looking into that now."

"That's great, Z. Really."

"Yes, I'm going to do it for Rocky. I'll let him run the whole shop and even allow him to come in as part owner just to set him up."

"Zenora, that's a wonderful gesture. Have you told him yet? He will be beside himself."

"No, I haven't. I want to get it for his birthday. That boy is my sweetheart. He definitely has my back and deserves an opportunity like this."

Rocky had been Z's ever-faithful office manager and assistant for years. As Nicole looked at him, she thought he resembled a younger version of the singer Prince. With his delicate features and big doe eyes, one would assume he played the submissive role in relationships, or the "bottom," as they say. Everyone believed Rocky when he talked about his escapades. He never said them in a boastful *Look, bitches I can get your man* kind of a way, but he shared them more like it was girl talk, and Nicole had often witnessed men waiting outside in their cars for Rocky.

Rocky would say, "Yes, I'm a queen, and I might dress femme, but I gotta dick, too, and I do more with it than pee. So if some man thinks he's just gonna flip me over and run up in me and I don't get my turn, his ass is crazy." Rocky was not one for role-playing when it came to sex.

"Hell, no, Ms. Nicky, I am an equal-opportunity employer here. We do everything equally or it don't get done. Unless, of course, it's LL Cool J. That *papi* could definitely have whatever he wants if he went that way."

Nicole had to agree with Rocky. Even at forty, LL could give a lesson or two to brothas on how to act, look, and perform, especially some of these younger rappers and Hollywood types that think they have it all. That it's just about them.

Zenora said, "It's so sad that so many hairstylists go from shop to shop and year to year, never really owning any more than what's in their styling case. No matter how good a hairstylist is, you won't find one who doesn't dream of opening his or her own shop. But the likelihood of that happening is slim. Most end up fifty-five years old, working two or three days in someone else's shop, dressing ridiculously, wearing outlandish makeup, and doing some heads on the side at their house just to make ends meet. I'm not going to let that happen to Rocky."

"You're a great boss, Z," Nicole said.

Zenora's voice took on an odd edge as she asked Nicole, "So, have you seen or spoken to Tisha?"

"Not in a few weeks," Nicole said. "Why?"

"Oh, no reason." Just as abruptly, Zenora changed the subject.

"You know, Nicky," Z said as she studied Nicole's head, "you really don't need that many more highlights put in."

"Really?"

"No, it will start to look fake. And besides people know that you get your hair done by me, so they would think I was crazy for putting more in."

Two

You Drive Me Crazy

S HE THOUGHT to herself that she didn't have a name anymore. She was just known as a crazy bitch, stupid woman, or ugly cow. Even she forgot her God-given name at times. It was Tisha Grant Perkins.

Roland's grip tightened around her neck. Tisha tried to calm herself down, but she started to slip into darkness.

"Look at me when I'm talking to you!" Roland's blaring voice commanded. His voice faded in and out, and Tisha wasn't sure if it was because she'd trained herself to tune him out or if she was losing her hearing after the many blows he had just delivered to her head. She forced her eyes open in order to obey his orders. "Why is it that you can't ever do what I ask you to do, huh? One simple fuckin' request, and you can't fuckin' do that!"

Tisha thought to herself, *Ask*? When did Roland ever ask her to do anything? He never even asked to marry her; he *told* her they were getting married.

"Why, Tish, why? I have told you time and time again, heavy starch in all my uniform shirts. And every week when you bring them back from the cleaners, it's the same shit! No fuckin' starch!"

He loosened his grip enough for her to be able to form words. "Ro-Roland, I—I told them to put *extra* starch in the shirts."

A tear ran down her cheek, which seemed to enrage him even more, and without warning he backhanded her across the face so hard, she flew across the room.

"What the hell is yo' ass cryin' for? It's my fuckin' shirt. I'm the one who should be cryin'. You crazy bitch!"

Tisha heard his footsteps come toward her, the hardwood floors in the bedroom magnifying the sound. She braced herself for more abuse, but instead, Roland knelt down and jerked her face around until their eyes met. Grasping Tisha's chin so roughly that her teeth hurt, he pulled his wife close.

"You know what? From now on, I'll take my own shirts to the fuckin' cleaners."

The scent of liquor on his breath was so strong, it momentarily paralyzed her. With his other hand, he softly brushed the hair out of her face. Tisha wished he wouldn't, because her hair blocked her vision. The less she saw of him, the better.

"I just want you to try and do better, that's all. That's

all I fuckin' want: for you to do better. Be the wife I married. Do you understand?"

Tisha nodded and promised that she would try harder.

Roland stared at her with tears welling up in his eyes and said, "I love you, girl," then gently kissed her on the lips.

Tisha had the urge to throw up but wouldn't dare—it would mess up his shirt.

Roland's cell phone rang, breaking his focus. He grabbed it from his pants pocket, and the expression on his face told his wife that he recognized the number.

"Yo, let me hit you right back." The caller was not satisfied with that answer, and Roland repeated his message more firmly: "*I said* I'll hit you right back." He slammed the phone shut.

Tisha figured that it must have been one of his many women and wondered if he treated them the way he did her. They probably got the royal treatment, and she got the job of taking his shirts to the cleaners.

He grabbed his keys off the dresser and walked out. Tisha couldn't move. No, of course, she *could* move; she just didn't want to. Lying between her bed and nightstand, she kept still. The sound of Roland descending the stairs grew more faint. Tisha counted all thirteen steps until he hit the landing. After hearing the front door open and close behind him, she listened for the sound of the lock turning. *He's gone.* Oh, how she wished he was really gone. Like *dead* gone.

No one would miss him; that's for sure. Well, maybe his

mother and sister, but maybe *not*. His mother had been bedridden for three months and was in the final stage of Alzheimer's. She didn't even know who *she* was, let alone her son. Grace, his sister, took care of her. Well, sort of.

Two weeks ago, Roland and Tisha drove to his mother's home to check on her condition. Tisha opted to stay inside the car because his visits usually lasted no longer than fifteen or twenty minutes. A short time after Roland entered the house, Tisha could hear his voice from outside, accusing his sister of neglecting their mother, whom he found wearing a urine-soaked diaper and lying on a bed stained with feces.

Grace argued, "She just got like that. If you don't like the way I take care of Ma, then you bring yo' faggot ass over here every day and take care of her, muthafucka!"

Grace got even louder, and Tisha assumed the whole neighborhood could hear the conversation. "What you think? I'm just s'pose to sit my ass up in the fuckin' house all day and not go out at all? You mus' be out yo' goddamn mind, nigga. I just went down to the fuckin' store to get my ass a pack of cigarettes."

"Well, why didn't you ask Mr. Manley next door to come over and watch her?" Roland yelled.

"I ain't got to ask nobody no muthafuckin' thing. Like I said, the bitch just peed. She was dry when I left for the store. Now if I ain't doing such a good fuckin' job, then you take the bitch over there to yo' house."

Tisha heard a door slam and wondered how many times the neighbors on this North Philadelphia street had witnessed all the ruckus that came out of the Perkins house. Carlisle Street was a very neat block in that crime-ridden area, and its residents took pride in their properties. Although many nearby streets had abandoned buildings, boarded-up homes, and drug traffic, Carlisle Street was definitely one of the exceptions. Many people cringed at the thought of living or working in North Philly, but there were quite a few blocks, like this one, where neighborhood respect and safety were high priorities and Clean Block posters and Neighborhood Watch signs were displayed on many of the corners. If there was one eyesore on Carlisle Street, it was the Perkins family home.

Melba Perkins had three children: Albert, Grace, and Roland. While Roland never said much about his child-hood, Grace once told Tisha after many glasses of whiskey that their brother, Albert, was shot and killed during a drug buy in 1998.

All three children had different fathers, who were absent in the home during their upbringing. "We didn't have any daddies, but we sure had a lot of 'uncles' in our lives. We had to stay in our rooms whenever an uncle came to the house. We knew they weren't no relations, just Momma's boyfriends," Grace said.

Their mother was a notorious numbers runner all the way up to her childrens' late teens. She delivered the win-nings and picked up the daily bets from customers in a ter-ritory assigned to her by Mr. Big. Melba earned the reputation as one of the best runners in his organization. Everyone was aware she carried money from the pickups, but thugs knew not to give Melba any trouble. Mr. Big didn't play nice if anyone attacked his workers or took his money. It was "hands off Melba," and that message was for the street thugs *and* the police. The numbers money fed and clothed the Perkins kids through most of their years before Alzheimer's took their mother's mind.

Tisha came from a different background than her husband did, but her love for him helped her to overlook their shortcomings. Early in their relationship, Grace joined Roland and Tisha at a local club for a friend's birthday party. It didn't take Tisha long to realize that she was in some rough company. The evening turned into a disaster when Grace got drunk and started a fight with one of the waitresses. That was her last and only outing with Grace Perkins.

Grace and Roland never did get along, although Grace did love her liquor and weed. All ninety-eight pounds and five feet of her was cutthroat, conniving, and downright mean. Plus her coarse attitude made it difficult for her to keep a job. But for some reason, she liked Tisha, which was rare, because Grace didn't like too many people, not even her brother.

"You're too good for Roland, 'n' what the fuck you see in that sad muthafucka, I'll never know." Grace resented Roland's bossiness and verbal attacks, but he was no match for her. All hell broke loose in that house whenever he stopped by, especially if she and Roland had liquor in them. Their mother always took Roland's side and left the cleaning, errands, and nursing tasks to Grace.

No matter how much Grace berated him, Roland always backed off. He definitely could dominate her physically with his six-foot, 225-pound frame, but the confrontations never went beyond words, although Tisha had seen Grace pull a knife on him after he accused her of stealing five dollars from his pocket. Roland believed his sister was on the pipe. Maybe. But Tisha definitely knew she smoked weed, because she picked up the smell when Grace hugged her the first time they met. It was so strong, Tisha almost got a contact high.

In a strange sort of way, Grace was her hero. She stood up to Roland—something Tisha could never do.

But Grace wasn't the only one who wondered why Tisha married Roland. She believed her friends thought the same thing, too, but Roland had come into her life at a time when she needed someone the most.

○ ○ ○

IT HAD BEEN a month after her father's death, and Tisha was prepared to spend another long night at work. Hunched over her desk, she was determined to get to the bottom of the never-ending pile of paperwork. She loved her job—she was a social worker, which was rewarding but emotionally draining and time consuming. But anything was better than being at home by herself, where everywhere she looked there was a reminder of her beloved daddy.

"Ahem." Someone stood at the doorway and cleared his throat to get her attention. "Miss Grant?" Tisha looked up and noticed her client, Roland Perkins, who needed social services for his mother, a victim of Alzheimer's. As usual, Roland didn't show up empty-handed. He clutched a bouquet of tulips, which he'd found out were Tisha's favorite.

"Roland!" she exclaimed, pleased for the break from the paperwork. "How nice to see you. But we didn't have an appointment today, did we?" Tisha glanced over at her calendar.

"Well, I thought I would surprise you. You've been so helpful to me and my family, and I wanted to take you out to dinner."

Tisha was confused and delighted. Roland wasn't much in the looks department, but he had a certain charm, and he was always so nice and respectful to her. She was tempted, but she didn't want to mix business with pleasure.

"That's awful kind of you, but—"

Roland cut her off. "Please, I insist. There's a new French bistro in Center City, and I took the liberty of making a reservation for us. Please let me do this for you?"

After thinking for a moment, Tisha relented and accepted Roland's invitation for dinner. "Okay, Roland, I'll join you. But could you give me at least an hour to finish up some last-minute paperwork? Why don't you go ahead, and I'll join you for a drink in a while."

"I don't mind waiting," Roland said with a twinkle in his eye. "I'll be in the lobby until you finish."

"Okay, fine. I shouldn't be too long," Tisha said with a weary smile.

As Roland turned to leave her office, Tisha watched

him. She couldn't help but laugh at herself. It had been so long since she'd had a date, let alone received flowers from a brotha. Something about Roland's confidence and take-charge personality intrigued her. How dare he just assume she'd say yes and automatically make reservatiõns for two? How did he know that she didn't already have a man who might not like another man bringing her flowers and invit-ing her out to dinner? She had certainly never discussed her personal life with him, but she had to admit, he did pique her interest.

By the time Tisha finished and went downstairs to meet Roland, more than an hour had passed—almost two, in fact. Tisha felt awful. Surely he had left by now. She planned to call him to apologize. But when she stepped off the elevator, there sat Roland, smiling and patiently waiting.

"I'm so sorry, Roland," Tisha said. "The paperwork on that case took much longer than I expected. I had no idea so much time had passed. Why didn't you come back up to the office?"

"It's okay. I don't mind," Roland assured her. "Besides, I called the restaurant and asked them to hold the reserva-tion for a little longer."

Midway through dinner, and about half a bottle of wine later, Tisha was relaxed enough that she had kicked off her pumps under the table. She felt more comfortable than ever before, and she and Roland were sitting a little closer together. The sound of her own laughter surprised her because it had been such a long time since she'd enjoyed herself like this. Sure, there were several nights out with the girls that were fun, but a woman has a different kind of laugh when she's with a man. And this man made her laugh. He seemed interested in her life, where she came from, what her dreams and goals were. And he listened—something that she felt many men didn't do, at least the ones she had dated. Usually it was only a matter of time before they were trying to get her in the sack. Tisha and Roland's perfect night was interrupted by an apologetic manager who informed them that unfortunately they would have to end their evening because it was closing time.

Tisha looked at her watch and couldn't believe so much time had passed. Had they really been sitting there for almost four hours? "Where is everyone?" Tisha remarked when she noticed they were the last ones left in the restaurant. She and Roland laughed, and feeling somewhat embarrassed, they excused themselves and left the restaurant.

While waiting for the valet to bring their cars, Tisha shivered at the chill night air and wished she had not left her sweater in the car. Noticing her discomfort, Roland immediately pulled off his jacket and wrapped it around her shoulders. He pulled her close in an innocent but inviting embrace, and Tisha welcomed it. It felt good to have a man's arms around her again. She thought for a moment as she tried to remember the last time this sort of thing happened or when she last felt like this. She couldn't recall either. Both cars arrived at the same time, and Roland took care of the tab.

"I'll follow you home to make sure you get there safely," Roland offered.

"Oh, that's all right. You don't have to," Tisha responded. "I'll be fine, but thank you for offering." True she'd had a lot of wine, but not enough to let a client and near stranger follow her home. Tisha smiled and hugged Roland tenderly before handing him his jacket. "Thank you, Roland, for a wonderful evening."

Driving home, Tisha realized that even though it was almost midnight, for some reason, she didn't feel tired at all. She even felt a little giddy. What was this feeling? she wondered. All the way home, she couldn't stop thinking of Roland—and that mesmerizing look on his face when he gazed at her. How could such a nice gentleman still be single? Granted, he was no Boris Kodjoe, but he wasn't Flavor Flav either.

Once she was settled in at home, she called Roland to let him know she'd made it back safely. Tisha joked, "Now you can turn your cell phone off."

"It's not my cell phone number that I gave you, but my home number," Roland said.

That impressed Tisha even more—she knew he wasn't a man playing games, and they ended up talking into the wee hours of the morning. That was totally out of the norm for Tisha Grant, behaving like some love-struck schoolgirl. She had to laugh.

It wasn't long before they became romantically involved. During their first time making love, Roland explored every inch of her body. It had been such a long time since anyone had touched her like that. Sure, she had "maintenance dates" or "touch-ups" as Zenora called them, but they were just that—hookups. Just enough to keep her motor running and feed certain needs, but that was it. With Roland, it was different. It was one thing to give your body to a man, but it was another when you relinquished your mind to him. Roland was her Mr. Right. And Tisha's life would never be the same.

When Tisha told Zenora she was dating one of her clients, Z told her not to bring any "sick puppies" home and to stop trying to cure the world. Tisha wished she had listened to her friend.

Roland began to show more undesirable traits—a sharp word here, a push or shove there—but the social worker in Tisha just tried to make things better or solve the problem. But there were some things and some people that couldn't be fixed. Besides, Roland filled a need. Tisha was reeling from her father's death, and Roland's strength, decisiveness, and take-charge nature had been comforting to her. At first.

Eventually Roland separated Tisha from all her friends and convinced her to quit her job. They got married and had a child together—a daughter, Kimmy—and he said he would take care of them both. Getting her hair done at Zenora's was cut down, too. Roland said she didn't need it. He didn't even want her to wear makeup or perfume; he said it was for whores, and besides, she was a natural beauty. But out of the corner of her eye, Tisha caught Roland straining his neck to ogle the cheapest-looking women. He did a good job on her, she admitted to herself—he'd divided and conquered. *But,* she thought, *I let him.*

Yesterday afternoon, Roland had pulled up in front of his family's home. Grace ran to the glass front door, and her big grin signaled that she was either drunk, high, or, less likely, simply glad to see them. She came out, and her attention went directly to Kimmy. "Dare go my sweet pooh bear. Come here to yo' auntie Grace."

Grace was missing more teeth than the last time Tisha had seen her, and her fingertips were dark—burnt-like, which usually happened when someone was on the crack pipe. *Maybe Roland is right,* Tisha thought. She had enough experience as a social worker to recognize the physical signs of drug addiction.

Roland brushed right by his sister without greeting her and went into the house to see their mother.

"Tisha girl, you let me know if you ever want me to watch Kimmy for you. That's if you gots somethin' to do."

A closer look at Grace revealed that her gums were as black as tar.

"Okay, thanks, Grace. I will," Tisha lied.

Within a few minutes, Roland came from behind and snatched Kimmy from his sister's arms. He was mad as ever. Not saying a word, he started the car and put it in drive. Grace was surprised and screamed at them all the way to the corner, "You need to bring yo' punk ass around here more often to see yo' mammy, bitch!"

Roland kept his eyes straight ahead while driving. Tisha

was silent for the remainder of the ride home. Even Kimmy sensed the tension and was unusually quiet the entire time in her car seat. There had to be something deep in his past that Grace knew about. Why did she hate her brother so, and why did he avoid her as much as possible? There had to be more to explain their volatile relationship than just her drug addiction.

○ ○ ○

MELBA PERKINS had had little time for her kids. She was too busy running the streets to worry about what they were doing. She'd actually never wanted kids anyway—it was just something that happened. Anytime Melba could pawn them off on someone else, she did so. But of all her children, Roland was the one she at least paid some attention to because he was the spitting image of his father. Out of all her men—and there were plenty—Melba loved only Frank Owens, who was a no-good street hustler. Frank was shot and killed at a craps game, and Melba was never the same after that. So by the time Roland was twelve years old and Grace was eight, they were pretty much on their own. Their fifteen-year-old brother, Albert, was away, serving his second stint in juvenile lockup.

Roland started acting out in school, so Melba enrolled him in an after-school program at St. Michael's, which was headed by the soft-spoken Brother Mills, a fortyish priest. Melba wasn't religious or trying to save her son's soul, but every time she got called in by a teacher or principal because of Roland's wreaking havoc, it cost her *money* and *time*—two things she could not spare. When you ran street numbers, it was an all-day affair that needed one's undivided attention.

Initially, Roland resented going to St. Michael's, because to participate in the program, he also had to attend Mass on Sundays. But after a while the benefits presented themselves. Roland was able to play basketball and dodgeball with the other boys and get free cookies and juice. Sometimes Brother Mills would even take the boys to the movies. Roland started spending more time at the church. He liked the white priest, and he soon found out that Brother Mills liked him, too—a little too much.

Roland didn't realize that Brother Mills was treating him a little differently from the other boys. Roland could do no wrong in Mills's eyes. Some of the other boys started to resent Roland—especially Travis, a fourteen-year-old who never missed an opportunity to bully Roland whenever Brother Mills wasn't around. Roland had no idea why Travis hated him so. It got to the point where he couldn't take the abuse anymore, so he told Brother Mills, and soon after that Travis was nowhere to be found. At first, Roland was glad that Travis was gone, but after seeing Travis around the neighborhood looking lost and bewildered, Roland began to feel bad. Sometimes on the way to the church, he'd see Travis sitting alone across the street from it. After a while people started talking about Travis being "on that stuff" because he was acting strangely and was always dirty. Even Melba had noticed the change in him, warning her kids, "Y'all stay away from that crazy-ass fool, Travis. That boy done lost his damn mind."

Brother Mills started buying Roland things like new Air Jordans and taking him to a Sixers game. After one game, it was so late that Brother Mills said it would be okay if Roland stayed with him at his apartment. He told Roland that he'd call his mother and tell her. Roland told him that there was no need to worry, because Melba probably wasn't home anyway. Roland was so tired by the time they arrived at the apartment that all he wanted to do was sleep. He immediately parked himself on the sofa and prepared for bedtime. Brother Mills told him that his bed was big enough and that they could share it. It would be like they were on a camping trip. Besides, his only television was located in his bedroom, and Brother Mills said he had something to show Roland that would have to be their secret—that only special friends of his got to see it.

As Roland lay on the bed, Brother Mills put in a videotape. Roland thought that they'd be watching a kung fu movie or maybe the new Eddie Murphy movie, *Beverly Hills Cop*. Instead, there were kids, some younger than him, doing all sorts of sexual things with adults. Roland didn't know why Mills wanted him to see this. Could it be his way of teaching Roland about the birds and the bees? It was all too confusing to him at the time, but he'd soon find out why. For now, he was too tired to care.

Brother Mills liked children. He'd start off with a pat on the shoulder, which would progress to a quick hug or embrace, each one longer than the last. Roland didn't mind. He trusted Brother Mills, who was like a father to him, and being with Brother Mills—and all it entailed— was better than being at home.

Grace resented Roland getting the opportunity to be away from home as much as he did. She wanted to go to St. Michael's, too. She'd noticed a change in Roland. When he did come home, he'd have new sneakers or a new baseball jersey. He seemed always to have money, which he'd share with her sometimes.

After dropping off Roland at school one morning, Brother Mills saw Grace. Roland told him that she was his little sister. Brother Mills commented on how cute she was. "Why don't you bring her over to play sometimes?" Mills asked.

"She'll just get in the way," Roland replied.

One day, after school, Melba, Roland, and Grace were having dinner together. It was a rare occurrence, and even though dinner was a frozen pizza and Kool-Aid, it was dinner nonetheless. "Take Grace with you over to the church gym when you go tonight," Melba ordered.

"Huh?" Roland asked, "Why?"

"Because I said so, that's why," Melba said, slapping him in the mouth. "I ask the questions around here, not you.

"And besides," Melba added, "Brother Mills said it was okay."

○ ○ ○

WHEN BROTHER MILLS opened the door of his apartment, the first thing Grace noticed was that he was wearing his priest's collar. Brother Mills greeted her warmly with a long hug as Roland watched. He told her how pretty she was and offered her some milk and cookies. Grace looked at Roland for permission, and he nodded his head that it was okay. It wasn't long before Grace was ready to leave. Brother Mills gave her a blond-haired doll to play with as he and Roland played a Nintendo game on the television. She was bored and ready to go, and when she told Roland, he said they would leave in a minute, but that she had to go to the bathroom before they left.

"I don't have to go," she said.

"Go anyway," her brother demanded.

When Grace finished in the bathroom, Roland was nowhere to be found.

"Where's my brother?" she asked Mills.

"Oh, he had to run an errand for me. I'll make sure you get home," Brother Mills said with a strange expression on his face, which made Grace feel uneasy.

Brother Mills told Grace to follow him into his bedroom because he had something to show her.

"I don't want to," Grace said.

"I thought you were a good girl, Grace," Brother Mills said. "And good girls do what adults tell them to. Do you want me to tell your mother that you were disobedient? Besides, Roland likes spending time in my bedroom."

Not wanting to risk Melba's wrath, Grace reluctantly followed Brother Mills.

Once in the room, Brother Mills asked Grace for a hug.

"But you already hugged me when I got here," Grace said, looking around.

"Grace, God wants you to listen to me and do what I

say," said Brother Mills. He reached for her hand and pulled her onto his lap.

Grace was scared and confused and started to cry.

"Now, hush, Grace," Brother Mills whispered as his hand traveled up Grace's skirt. "God doesn't like little girls who cry, and you are making God unhappy and sad."

Grace tried not to cry, because she didn't want God to get mad at her.

That's all she remembered until she woke up. Brother Mills was washing her with a soapy towel. There was blood on the bed, and her school uniform was spread out on a chair. Now fully awake, she felt a sharp pain "down there." She thought to herself, *Wait until I tell Roland what Brother Mills did to me. He'll kick his ass—church man or not!*

Brother Mills told Grace to get dressed and to keep what had happened a secret between them. He told her he was disappointed in her, and so was God, because she'd cried. "Roland never cried," Brother Mills admonished. "Not even once."

When Grace got home, she went straight to Roland's room. She told her brother what had happened, but he accused her of lying. "Brother Mills would never do anything like that," he said, angry at her.

"Why did you leave me there?" Grace pleaded.

"I thought you wanted to stay and play with the stupid doll," he told her.

Grace started to cry, and Roland told her to stop being a baby and go to bed and that she would be all right in the morning. As Grace turned to leave Roland's room, she noticed a hundred-dollar bill on his dresser.

"Where'd you get that from?" Grace asked.

"Brother Mills gave it to me, and you better not tell Mom," he warned.

Grace just stared at him.

"Don't worry," Roland said. "I'mma give you some."

Grace didn't want any of it, and she walked out the room. She hated God, Brother Mills, but most of all, she hated Roland.

Your big brother was supposed to protect you, right? Not lead you into hell.

○ ○ ○

MAYBE THE ALTERCATION yesterday with Grace was why Roland was so angry this morning about his starched shirts. Tisha, as she usually did, tried to rationalize his anger: It could be his job, his mother's illness, his sister's attitude, maybe his other woman. But, Tisha did know one thing for sure: She was no longer in control of herself.

My depression has set in so deep that it's found a permanent home in my soul. When did my life become such a mess?

Nicole had once suggested to Tisha that she might be experiencing postpartum depression, but what did she know? *Nicole's no doctor,* Tisha thought. *She might be marrying one, but she doesn't know what she's talking about.* Tisha knew her depression did not stem from her baby. Hell no! Kimmy was the one bright light in her life.

Her daughter was her one reason to get up in the morning. Tisha hadn't always been this way. She was always positive and enjoyed life. Her daddy used to say that if there was but "one ounce of good in a person," Tisha would find it.

Tisha still missed her daddy. There wasn't a day that went by that she didn't think of him. He was her champion. Losing her father four years ago after his long battle with prostate cancer was a heartbreaking blow. Even in the last stages of the cancer, he was strong, never complained or gave in. Her daddy held strong to the very end.

She vaguely remembered her mother, who was killed by a hit-and-run driver while crossing City Line Avenue. Tisha was only three years old when it happened, and from what she has been told, her mother was hailing a taxi from the Bala Cynwyd Mall. She stepped too far into the street, and then a vehicle made a sudden illegal turn, knocking her in the air. Her mother died on impact, and the driver was never caught.

Witnesses told police they saw a white female driver with blond hair in a dark-colored car speed away after the impact. She had to have known she hit something or someone, because she slowed down at the next traffic light and glanced back very briefly, long enough for pedestrians to get a few letters from her license plate. The police never bothered to pursue it, and the accident got only five lines in the *Philadelphia Daily News*.

The family always suspected that if Tisha's mother had been a person of prominence, an arrest would have been made. Her grandmother told Tisha that a few days after the accident, her father received a cashier's check in the amount of three thousand dollars from an unknown source. Her father was furious. He thought it was blood money from the driver or someone who knew about the accident. It could have been a donation from a concerned party, but her father sensed something different. Granny said that he tore the check in a hundred pieces and didn't want to pursue the matter any further. It just would not bring his wife back.

But her mother wasn't forgotten. Tisha's father shared photographs and stories about her mother and kept the memory of her alive. In her childhood home, there were family pictures in every room, and her mother was in most of them.

Everyone in the neighborhood loved Tisha's father, Gus Grant. When she was a young girl, all of Tisha's friends told her they wished their dads were like hers. Since her mother wasn't around to teach her girly things, her grandmother took over that role. But her father wanted the primary role of raising her. He learned how to braid hair, taught her to cook, and even showed Tisha how to sew. She remembered that her father's rough thick fingers could barely thread a needle.

Late one night, she got up to go to the bathroom, and there was a light on in her father's room. She peeked in, and he was still trying to thread that needle to sew her Girl Scout Brownie outfit. He could barely keep his eyes open. He was so tired, but he was determined. He hated to fail at anything. Tisha crept away quietly because she knew that if he saw her spying, he would be embarrassed. When she opened her eyes that next morning, there hanging on the closet door was her uniform, ready to wear.

When Tisha was nine, Nicole, Freda, Mira, and the other girls used to come over frequently because her father gave them so much attention. Mira said she was going to marry her father, so Tisha decided she didn't like her anymore and Mira could no longer be her friend. That was her daddy, and she didn't like sharing him.

Tisha's father enrolled her in the Girl Scouts, dance classes, and piano lessons. No matter how busy he got at the Acme Plant, he made it to every recital and program. Sometimes at night when they'd return from an event, she'd hear him in his room quietly crying because he missed his wife and was sad that she wasn't there with him to share in his pride at their daughter.

One morning at breakfast, Tisha asked if he loved her mother more than her, and if he cried for her when she wasn't near him. That was the only time she thought she hurt her father. Not necessarily because of what she said, but because she referred to her mother as *her*.

"She's your mother! And if you don't want to call her Mom, then you call her Mrs. Grant, but she is never to be referred to as *her* again."

"I'm sorry, Daddy. I didn't mean anything by it."

"Well, you ought to watch what you say before you say it, young lady. Go to your room."

Embarrassed and hurt, Tisha replied, "Yes, sir."

Later that evening, like clockwork, her father came to tuck her in and read a bedtime story.

"It's okay, Daddy. I don't deserve a story tonight. You can just tuck me in."

He said with a soft smile, "What am I going to do with you, girl? Remember, I love you and Momma both the same."

"What did you say, Daddy?"

"I said, I love you and Momma the same."

"Oh," she replied.

He followed his routine by reading her favorite bedtime story, *The Little Engine That Could,* for the hundredth time.

When he left her room, Tisha reached for the framed photograph of her family from the nightstand, then placed it on her pillow and silently vowed never to hurt her father like that again.

Her Barbie doll would have to remain on the nightstand alone that night.

Her father never remarried, and even though there were a few women he dated, he never brought them to their house. When Tisha got older, he told her he never married out of respect for her mother. "And besides," he said, "there would have been no woman allowed to come here and you not give her hell, Tisha."

Tisha couldn't dispute that.

○ ° ○

LYING HERE on the floor of her bedroom today, face swollen and neck bruised, Tisha knew her father would be disappointed in her.

The sound of Kimmy crying snapped her back to reality.

She pulled herself up from the floor and went to her child. Looking at her beautiful baby in her crib, she was so glad Kimmy didn't resemble Roland in any way. Yes, Kimmy was the spitting image of Tisha. Things were not that bad after all.

One day I'll tell Daddy's spirit that I'm sorry.

Three

I Am Woman, Hear Me Roar

DENISE UPSHAW had just seen her last client for the day at the firm. She was supposed to be hosting Nicole's bachelorette party at Mira's Loose Balloon club, but a major water pipe had burst in the club's basement, and to her disappointment, Nicole's apartment was to be used instead. Denise was aggravated because she wanted everything in place for the special event, and the club would have been a perfect location. However, she had to admit that she was a little relieved. Originally, she didn't want to have Nicole's party at the Loose Balloon. She relented only because of persuasion from the other girls. It wasn't because it was a gay club; that didn't bother her at all. She just didn't feel it was a classy enough venue for someone of her prominence to host any kind of affair.

Denise assured herself that even with this unexpected

turn of events, the gift she planned for Nicole would top everyone else's. Through her connections, she was able to secure two first-row concert tickets and backstage passes for R & B singing sensation Ginuwine, at the Merriam Theatre. Ginuwine had been one of Nicole's favorite singers since he released his first solo song, "Pony," in the 1990s. Denise shook her head, remembering when Nicole first saw Ginuwine. She'd called all the girls, screaming and demanding that they immediately turn on BET to see this fine brotha's video. Getting those tickets was no easy feat, but Denise was friendly with one of Ginuwine's attorneys and managed to get the hookup—an expensive hookup! But Nicole was her girl, and she didn't mind the expense. But before she could head over to the party, Denise first had to make a stop at her Broad Street campaign headquarters to see how the painters were coming along.

○ ○ ○

SINCE ANNOUNCING her candidacy for city council in the First District, Denise had been doing triple duty—working at the law firm, raising campaign funds through public appearances, and perfecting her platform. If elected—better yet, *when elected*—one of the first things she would introduce was a bill prohibiting smoking in all public establishments, which had been one of her pet peeves since college. She knew that winning this campaign would be an uphill battle because the incumbent occupying the First District seat had been there for many terms, but Denise had a number of new plans for her district as well as for the city, and it was time for new blood in city council.

Judges from all four local courts—Traffic, Family, Municipal, and Common Pleas—held her in high regard, and she had a fine reputation and some backing from powerful politicians and union bosses. All she needed now were their endorsements and their money.

One of her campaign strategies was to court the Hispanic vote. Zenora was more than willing to make connections, and she got help from two of her Hispanic salon employees and lovers. Zenora also spoke Spanish and was available as Denise's interpreter at the weekly community meetings held at the Lighthouse Community Center, which was in a largely Hispanic neighborhood. Once word traveled through the neighborhood, Denise had quite a following.

Denise knew that Zenora's interest in helping her went beyond their being girls; Z was able to meet more of the Hispanic male population, thus keeping her options open for new *papis*.

Residents came to Denise with problems that she could easily handle through her contacts at City Hall, and if there were problems she couldn't handle, she gave them a referral to the proper agency or another lawyer in her law firm. The firm always took a few pro bono cases for needy families if Denise persisted. The city's leading Hispanic publication, *Al Día,* gave Denise's popularity a boost when it did a feature story on her weekly meetings and involvement in Philadelphia's Hispanic issues. She met new friends and volunteers who were willing to work at her campaign headquarters and do the necessary groundwork.

Denise often visited the city council chambers on the

fourth floor of City Hall. When the room was empty, security staff let her walk in for a brief period. Denise would sit quietly on the sideline benches reserved for the public spectators and visualize herself sitting at the leather-top oak desk reserved for the First District council member. Denise imagined that many embattled sessions took place during its one-hundred-plus years of meetings, protests, and budget hearings. Denise wanted to be a part of it. "I'm going to be sitting in that seat after the November election," she would say to herself aloud.

Denise parked in front of her campaign headquarters and marveled at the large red, white, and blue banner: ELECT ATTY DENISE UPSHAW TO 1ST DISTRICT COUNCIL.

"What are you doing? That is not the color I selected. The walls are supposed to be mint green, not forest green!" Denise yelled upon entering her campaign headquarters.

The painters were limited to only a few words of English, so they muttered something in Spanish. The two men smiled at her then continued painting.

"Stop! *Alto!*" Denise said. "*No mas*. Just stop! It's not right! I need you both to stop. Where is Domenick?"

The younger of the two responded, "*Sí*, Señor Domenick not here, gone home. You like color?"

"No, I don't like the color!" Denise reached for her cell phone and scrolled down the screen to Domenick's name.

"Oh, great—his voice mail. . . . Hi, Domenick, it's Denise Upshaw. Listen, I need you to call me immediately on my cell phone. I'm at my campaign office, and your painters are using the wrong color. I asked for mint green, not this forest green they're putting on my walls. It's too dark. I am sending them home. I expect you to have someone here bright and early tomorrow morning with the correct color to finish the job. And if you are not going to be here, let me suggest that you leave someone here that can speak English. Thank you, and good-bye."

The two workers knew enough English to realize that they had made some sort of drastic mistake, and they packed up their supplies to leave. Denise assumed they were father and son by their similar features and body build. As they passed her, the older gentleman said, "I sorry."

For a moment, Denise felt ashamed of the way she had reacted. They would be out of a job if Domenick replaced them, but she quickly dismissed that thought because nothing came before the election. Compromise, incompetence, and foolish mistakes couldn't be tolerated now. She checked her watch, turned off the lights, then locked the door behind her.

Since she didn't have time to go home and change, she made a quick trip to the restroom, where she double-checked her hair and makeup. The charcoal gray skirt with a silk fuchsia blouse skimmed her tall, lean frame. Her cell phone rang. She assumed it would be Domenick, but it was Renee.

"Hi, Denny. It's Ree Ree."

Denise hated when Renee referred to her as Denny, and she had no idea where her friend had gotten that from.

"Hey, Renee, what's up?" Denise said, not bothering to hide the annoyance in her tone.

"Gosh, girl, did I call at the wrong time? Are you okay?"

"No, no, Renee. I'm fine. Just a little frazzled about the way this campaign is going. What's going on?"

"I just tried Nicky at the house, and no one is picking up. Can you let her know my train is delayed and once I arrive at Thirtieth Street Station, I'll get a taxi right over?"

"Okay, no problem, I will. Sorry I answered the phone in such a negative tone. It's just that I've had one eventful day."

"It's okay, Denny. Feel better, and I'll see you when I get there. *Ciao, bella.*"

Denise left the headquarters and got in her gold BMW 645i convertible. As she headed toward Nicole's condo, she wished she had not offered to host this bachelorette party, because, at this moment, what she really wanted to do was go home, take a nice hot bath, turn off the phones, put on some John Legend, and go to bed.

Wishful thinking.

Just then her cell phone rang again. Another crisis.

Four

Sing a Song

TWO DAYS AGO, Nicole had gasped as she watched Freda try on her bridesmaid dress. Freda looked in the mirror and admired her body. Nicole let each one of her bridesmaids select her own style of dress for the wedding. As long as it was cream-colored, they could design the dress any way they wanted. And Freda's dress showed everything but her birth date. The front had a deep cleavage cut all the way down to Freda's waist and the length was so short, anyone could see Clara. (That's what Nicole's nana called a vagina. She called it either Clara or yo' pock-e-book.)

"Yeah, girl, I do look good, right?" Freda said, assuming that it was a gasp of approval.

Freda was named after the 1970s singer, Freda Payne, of "Band of Gold" fame. Free-spirited Freda was always the performer and "onstage." Life was Freda's stage.

Nicole rolled her eyes and bit her tongue. It was too late to add any fabric to the dress at this point, so she was just going to let Freda be Freda.

"Yeah, girl, you look good. But you already knew that," she teased.

Freda was a talented girl. Talk about singing. Oh, my God. Picture Whitney and Mariah rolled up in one. Yes—looks, talent, body. Freda had it all, except for that successful career she had always yearned for. Nicole couldn't understand why Freda hadn't been picked up by a label, but she suspected it was probably because Freda kept getting in her own way and falling for the wrong men all the time.

Freda loved her some B-boys, hood boys, and definitely any man with the thug look. If they had a criminal past, they were usually "fine as shit," according to Freda. And her men were always between twenty-one and twenty-five—that's how she liked them. If they didn't come with drama, she was not happy. Nicole couldn't count the times that Freda had had to bail out one of those jerks for some dumb shit they had gotten themselves into. But no matter how many times they'd do her wrong and have her go through crying spells, she'd be right back for more of the same with another new one. Freda was searching for something—and Nicole wasn't quite sure what it was—but wasn't everybody, in some way or another?

Freda received little or no support from her family when it came to her career choice. Both her parents were Witnesses, as in Jehovah, and were totally against her singing and her lifestyle. Because of that, she didn't bother much with either of them.

As Freda took the dress off, Alicia Keys's song "Fallin'" came on. Nicole braced herself because Freda could be negative when it came to other female singers, and Alicia was a frequent target of hers. "Oooh, I hate that girl!" Freda said, sucking her teeth. "You know she only made it because of Clive Davis." Clive Davis was the record mogul behind numerous successful female vocalists, including Whitney Houston.

"Hell, if I had the same opportunity, I would be where she is and maybe further," she said. "And don't let me get started on Beyoncé. She's just another chicken head who's standing in my way."

"Freda, I like Beyoncé," Nicole said. "You're sounding like a hater."

"Humph," Freda snorted. "What is there to hate on?"

Before Freda's mother, Lillian, became a Jehovah's Witness, she was a singer. Her biggest claim to fame was as lead backup singer for Teddy Pendergrass. As a matter of fact, on the evening of his infamous near-fatal car accident in 1982, Freda's mom and two other girls were following his car on the road. Rumor had it that she and Teddy were an item for a short time. Who knew for sure? Yet that was the extent of her career.

Today Lillian sang at the Kingdom Hall. Nicole had heard her sing. If there were a sing-off battle between Freda and her mother, Moms would win. In the late '80s, Lillian was the backup singer for another Philly superstar, Patti LaBelle, who graciously handed over the mic to Lillian one time too many.

Lillian started smelling her own pee. Instead of appreciating Patti for giving her the opportunity to show off her vocal skills, Lillian began making statements like, "Patti better watch out, 'cuz I'm coming for her!" Now Lillian was good, but when talking about Diva LaBelle, that was crazy talk. When Patti hit her stride, which was always, she took no prisoners. It taught Miss Lillian a lesson and broke her spirit, which was probably why she didn't want an entertainment career for her daughter. One by one, Miss Lillian began to lose all her contacts with the industry. Calls weren't returned; work dried up.

Looking at Freda's mom, it was obvious that at one time she was a stunning creature. Her demons were the streets, fast living, and men. All of those played a part in beating her up mentally and physically. She felt she had to make a choice—God or suicide. She chose God. Along came Mr. Henry, the only man in the neighborhood who bothered to pursue her despite her tarnished reputation, plus take on a daughter to care for. But he loved Lillian that much to marry her and embrace the role of stepdad to Freda.

Over the years, Lillian kept in contact with one person from her old life, a true friend for whom she named her daughter, the real Freda Payne. Ms. Payne was once an inspiration to Lillian.

Like so many faithful converts, Lillian judged everyone else and how they lived, especially her daughter, Freda.

Five

Memories Light the Corner of My Mind

WHEN NICOLE WAS about eleven or twelve years old and lived on Titan Street in South Philly, one of her best friends was a girl named Adrienne Ward. She was rail-thin, with a rich, deep chocolate complexion, and Nicole thought she was absolutely beautiful. In fact, she wanted to look just like her. She had this air of confidence that Nicole lacked. She was Miss Thing, and no one could tell her she wasn't.

Neighborhood kids teased Adrienne all the time about her dark skin and short hair. One kid called her "a dirty-headed tennis ball." Adrienne would nudge Nicole and laugh even harder than they did. Nicole wondered if she should have laughed, too. Since Adrienne was laughing, then it must be okay, she thought. So she joined in.

However, one day at Benson Elementary School, there was an experience that would haunt Nicole forever.

First, you had to know the neighborhood. Benson is in the heart of South Philly, where every girl living on the west side of Broad Street knew double Dutch.

The Mummers Parade on New Year's Day was portrayed as a South Philly tradition, but that was strictly on the east side of Broad—the white side. There wouldn't be any black folks out in the cold weather watching that event. In fact, black folks shunned it for years because some string bands wore black face makeup and depicted African Americans as comic buffoons. Nicole's father said the parade was a time for white men to dress up in feathers and get drunk. Blackface in the parade was eventually banned, but it remained a bitter pill among many Philadelphia blacks.

Benson School had the dodgeball and double Dutch titles. Team competitions at school and in different neighborhoods were commonplace. Each summer, the city's Department of Recreation held a double Dutch competition. Those girls at Tenth and Ritner never could touch the Benson girls, and that double Dutch team at St. Bart's was just sad. Rasheeda, one of the Benson stars, had a sprained ankle that year, but the school still won. Channel 10 featured the school on the evening news as they received trophies. Benson was *b-a-d*. Nicole's mother and father still displayed her trophy on the fireplace mantel.

No one could beat Adrienne at double Dutch. She was the team's very best. No matter how hard you tried—

forget it! That was her game. That child could jump some rope!

Maxine, an older girl by three years, lived one block from Nicole and Adrienne. She challenged Adrienne to a double Dutch duel. The one who jumped the fastest and the longest would be "the best gun" in double Dutch.

Nicole laughed because everyone in the neighborhood knew Adrienne's reputation as the queen of double Dutch.

It was like a scene in a cowboy movie. The fastest gun-slinger and the new rival would duel it out on the corner of Twenty-seventh and Wharton. In this case, their quick feet and agile moves would be their choice of weapons.

News spread throughout the school and nearby streets: "Maxine's gonna take on Adrienne, on Fridee after school on the Twenty-seventh Street lot."

By that afternoon, curiosity seekers—young and old—gathered on the empty lot to see the competition, and they circled Rasheeda and One Mo' Sandwich Terri, who handled the rope work. One Mo' Sandwich Terri got that nickname from the kids at school because she looked like if she ate one more sandwich, she'd be fat. Yet Rasheeda and One Mo' were champion jumpers and good friends. Frog-Eye Franny brought her mother's big pink bedroom alarm clock from home to time the action.

Maxine went first. She jumped like she was runnin' for her life with her tongue hanging out. She made Nicole's head spin. That tongue-hanging-out was something black girls did when they *knew* they were doing their thing! It's the same as when a sistah from South Philly was gettin' down on the dance floor—and she knew she was throwin' down. Every eye in the room would be on her. She was workin' hard: then that tongue came out—a symbol of confidence and an *I know I'm killin' it* attitude.

After heavy-paced nonstop jumping, Maxine was done. Sweat streamed down her cheeks, her hair stuck out like she was electrocuted, heavy wet rings of sweat came through her blue school uniform, and her knee-high white socks gathered around her ankles like loose rubber bands. She knew she'd nailed it. Franny shouted, "Two minutes and twenty-eight seconds."

Cheers came up from the crowd, which only drew more onlookers. Even a police patrol car stopped to see what the commotion was all about.

Next up was Adrienne. Nicole shouted, "Go, Adrienne!"

Her friend wore an expression of sheer determination and focus. Rasheeda and One Mo' Sandwich Terri started the count, "five, six, seven, eight . . ." as the "queen of jump" swayed back and forth to get the rhythm of the rope before leaping in. Nicole couldn't believe her eyes. She had never seen Adrienne jump like that. Like there was some sort of grand prize to be won. But there was. She was protecting her invisible crown of Double Dutch Queen of South Philly and the continued adoration from the neighborhood.

Rasheeda and One Mo' put the pepper to the ropes as Adrienne's black legs moved at bionic speed. Maxine's face started to contort. She looked possessed, and her nervous look resembled that of a hooker in church at Sunday-morning prayer service.

Adrienne had clearly exceeded the speed and time Maxine spent on the ropes. All eyes went to Franny and that big pink clock. She looked at the big black numbers, her frog eyes popping even larger. "Three minutes fifteen seconds!"

The crowd screamed, applauded, and Nicole roared along with everyone.

While Adrienne received accolades from the spectators, Maxine abruptly burst from the sidelines, pulled the rope, and shouted, "That bal'-headed bitch ain't beat me. Look at her. Hair so fuckin' short, her momma got to roll it up with rice!"

Only a few people giggled. But Nicole didn't. The crowd was aware Maxine was embarrassed she'd ever called the challenge, and she was a poor loser. Rasheeda and One Mo' gathered the jump rope and moved away to avoid any further confrontation; Frog-Eye Franny ran home with her mother's big pink bedroom clock.

If my parents heard me use that language, I'd be dead, Nicole thought. She wasn't going to laugh at the teasing, even if Adrienne laughed, too, or even if she nudged her to do so. But Adrienne didn't even make a sound. Tears formed in her eyes as she picked up her schoolbooks and slowly walked through the quiet crowd toward home.

Maxine stood triumphant, as if she just won. *Didn't my girl just slaughter her in this match?* Nicole thought. The wrong person was crying. Nicole followed Adrienne down Twenty-seventh Street to give her some support and let her know she'd rather be a dark sweet chocolate with no hair, thank you, than be a cross-eyed loser like Maxine, who saw two of everything.

"Nicole girl, you are crazy. I ain't thinkin' 'bout Maxine Hamilton. She ain't only cross-eyed, she smells like cat pee. So there!"

Nicole and Adrienne laughed so hard, they had to sit on the nearest front steps to compose themselves. Unfortunately, they landed on Miss Ethel's white marble front steps—her pride and joy. Everyone respected that small sign in her window: NO STANDING, SITTING, OR SPITTING ON MY STEPS. Hopefully, she wouldn't chase them away, but they just couldn't walk any farther. Giggling overtook the girls. Soon, though, Adrienne's voice softened as she became more serious, "But I do wish I was as pretty as you are, Nicky."

"What? Why?"

"You remind me of Hilary Banks," she said.

Nicole snapped, "Who wants to look like her?"

"Me!" Adrienne snapped right back. "I look at the *The Fresh Prince of Bel-Air* every week just to watch her. Yeah, she might be ditzy, but you light-skin girls get all the attention from boys, the teachers call on you first, and you get to be in the front line of all the class pictures. Me? I have to jump rope and sweat to get my attention."

Nicole was stunned and didn't know what to say for two reasons: What Adrienne said was true, and she was embarrassed for having light skin.

"We are sisters to the end, Nicole. I'm gonna be at your wedding, and you're gonna be at mine."

"Yeah, like 'Ebony and Ivory' from the Stevie Wonder–Paul McCartney song."

Nicole told Adrienne how her mother played that song a lot. Her mother wasn't crazy about Paul McCartney, but she loved Stevie Wonder and said, "That little blind black boy got some talent!" But in any case, her mother had everyone in the house humming that tune over and over. Nicole's father was hoping the tape would break.

"I want to be Ebony," Nicole proclaimed.

"Girl, you can't be no Ebony. You too light," Adrienne said. "I'll be Ebony; you can be Ivory."

The next day Nicole went by Adrienne's house so that they could walk to school as they did every day. No one answered the door. This was strange because Raja, the family dog, was pacing back and forth at the front window. There was no answer, so Nicole turned to leave. Raja was whimpering in the front window to get her attention.

Nicole tapped on the window. Still no answer. If she waited around any longer, she'd be late for school, and Miss Jones did not play that. Getting marched down to the principal's office was Nicole's worst nightmare.

All during Nicole's classes, Adrienne was on her mind. And where was Mrs. Ward? Why hadn't she answered the door? Nicole couldn't focus on her schoolwork, and she had a math test that day, too. She couldn't wait to get out after the dismissal bell blared. Nicole hauled her tail to Titan Street. Adrienne lived only four doors up from her. Nicole banged on the door and shouted, "Adrienne! Adrienne, are you home?"

Mrs. Ward answered the door and took what seemed

a lifetime before she spoke—long enough for Nicole to realize just how much her daughter resembled her—dark chocolate and very pretty.

Mrs. Ward spoke so softly through the front glass door that Nicole had to strain to understand her. "Adrienne's in the hospital, Nicole."

"The hospital!" Butterflies fluttered in Nicole's stomach, which always happened when she was nervous or scared.

When Nicole's uncle Paul got nervous about stuff, he would laugh and say, "Those suckas be flying all over in every direction 'n' you gotta get 'em to all fly in one direction. They'll settle down. Just close your eyes and concentrate, puddin'."

But her uncle Paul's cure wasn't working this time. Those butterflies in Nicole's stomach had a mind of their own, and they were not listening to her. She didn't like them that much, and she wanted them to fly out.

"I only came home to get some things for her, and then I'm on my way back to the hospital, Nicole," Mrs. Ward said.

"What happened?" Nicole's butterflies were going crazy now.

"She had another attack, baby. The doctors said she must have overdone it yesterday. Were you girls playing too hard at recess? It was very hot yesterday, and Adrienne knows that with her condition, she needs to find some shade, sit down, and relax." Adrienne suffered from asthma and epileptic seizures, but she never talked about her illnesses.

"We just jumped some rope, that's all, Mrs. Ward, but she was okay because we walked home together. Can I go and see her?"

"Not today, baby. Maybe tomorrow if she's up to it. Then your mother can bring you by after school."

Mrs. Ward touched Nicole's saddened face, and Nicole sensed that Adrienne was in greater pain than she could imagine. Why had Adrienne let Maxine push her into that silly challenge? All over a stupid jump rope game.

"Okay, well, tell her to hurry up home."

"She'll be fine, Nicole. I'm sure she wants to be right back here with her best friend. Both of you will be laughin' and playin' again real soon. Don't worry."

◦ ◦ ◦

ADRIENNE'S FUNERAL was gloomy, but she looked so peaceful in her casket. Nicole, her mother, and her nana sat in the church to pay their respects. Nicole's father didn't want her to attend the funeral at all, because he believed children couldn't understand the full meaning of the funeral ceremony and death. But Nicole's mother won that debate: "That's her best friend who passed away. One day she may regret not saying good-bye."

One by one, young and old, friends and family took their places behind the church microphone to say how sweet Adrienne was, how funny she was, how nice she was.

Just as I said what I wanted to say about my friend, who should walk in but Maxine! She knew better than to sit with Nicole's class and double Dutch team. Their heads were down in prayer, but Nicole passed the message about Maxine's arrival. She was sitting in the back with her ol' cross-eyed self, crying, and making all that ridiculous noise. She only did it for attention. The team made sure she saw their dirty looks. Nicole rolled her eyes so far back in her head, she got a headache! *She probably sees two caskets,* Nicole thought, *two Adriennes. Good.*

The autopsy revealed that Adrienne had had an epileptic seizure and asthma attack. Both occurring at the same time were too much for her heart. She never came out of her coma. Nicole's friend went to a place where they say everything is better. Where everyone loves one another and no one is judged on how they look. Nicole was angry that Adrienne had left her. Hadn't they pledged they would be friends to the end? Well, was this the end? From that day forward, Nicole never again took a friend for granted.

○ ○ ○

SHE DROVE INTO the underground parking structure of her condo building in the upscale Rittenhouse Square neighborhood, and Nicole caught a glimpse of herself in the rearview mirror. She looked good! Once again, Zenora had worked her magic. Her hairstyle—a shoulder-length layered bob with honey-colored highlights—was the bomb.

Nicole had grown up only blocks away from the Square, but it seemed like a million miles away when she was a child. She'd walk through the Square with her mother on their way to shop at Wanamaker's department store on Market Street and would always wonder what those people did to be able to live in the magnificent high-rise buildings. She rarely saw any black people and later learned that the Square was once an exclusive neighborhood for old-moneyed white Philadelphia families, and that blacks had had to arrive and leave through the back entrances until a few decades ago. And now, here she was, a successful investment banker with her very own place on the Square.

Nicole took the elevator from the garage to the nineteenth floor and entered her showroomlike apartment. She walked into the living room and sat down on her chocolate brown L-shaped plush sofa. Its peach-colored throw pillows matched the walls, which were graced by original pieces of African American art by Romare Bearden and Elizabeth Catlett. Oriental rugs were placed throughout the rooms of her home, enhancing the glistening hardwood floors.

She glanced toward her dining area as she thought about tonight's party. An oblong mahogany-and-cherry-wood table with seating for eight was in the center of the room. On it sat a large Waterford crystal vase of fresh white gladioli and calla lilies. The bouquet filled the air with a hypnotic fragrance.

She was proud of her two-bedroom, one-and-a-half-bath townhome. It represented all she had accomplished in her career, and while she was happy to be moving to the next stage of her life, she had a fleeting sense of losing a part of herself. But she was ready to move on. Alan was building them a home from the ground up in Lower

Merion, an exclusive suburban area on Philly's Main Line. She and Alan had discussed whether to keep the condo or rent it out, but in the end, they'd decided to sell it. She figured she would get two million dollars for the prime space. Real estate on the Square in Philadelphia was always high market.

Nicole thought about her mother's reaction when she told her that Alan had asked her to marry him. Her mother had nearly fainted. "Thank you, Jesus," she testified, "because girl, you had me wondering if I was going to live long enough to see my baby married and have some kids."

"Mom, you're only fifty-three years old," Nicole laughed. "It's not like you're eighty-one and in a wheelchair."

Hell, Nicole thought, *I didn't plan on waiting till thirty-one to get married. It just sort of happened that way.* She'd been close several times.

There was Jerry, a football coach, whom she'd met at one of Denise's parties at her law firm. They had a lot in common, and she fell hard for his ass, too. But he was confused and insecure about everything. He was twenty-nine and divorced for the second time when they'd met. That should have been a warning sign right there. But when do women in love really pay attention to warning signs?

Everyone thought they were the perfect couple, but after spending more than two on-and-off years with him, she realized that Jerry, no matter how hard he tried, would never be able to love her fully. He might have been sweet— with a big heart and an even bigger tool—but he didn't love himself.

And he didn't have a clue about making love. Every woman wants to make love, and every woman wants to have great sex some time in her life, and Jerry couldn't deliver either.

But the final straw was that he was a momma's boy. His mother constantly meddled in his entire life, and that extended to Nicole. Any discussion of his mother's interference was totally off-limits. Nicole spent his thirtieth birthday in Cancún with him *and* his mother—that's right, his mother shared a connecting suite with them the entire time.

It was there that he'd asked Nicole to marry him. And she almost accepted, but the words that came out of her mouth were, "I can't, because I'd be marrying you *and* your mother." That was a long and quiet flight back, and Nicole always got the impression that Gladys was gloating in the seat behind her on the return flight. Jerry broke up with her right there after the plane landed in the Philadelphia airport, and they never spoke again.

Then there was Lamont Davidson, a six-foot-four-inch copper-toned, cocky dreamboat—who turned out to be a classic jerk! He stayed in front of the mirror more than most women. They met in a club.

Nicole's first mistake was meeting a man on singles night in a club. A man in that environment was not there to meet a significant other or a potential wife. He was there because he's single and wanted to remain that way. Duh! Nicole shook her head at the memory. *When are we going to learn?* she thought to herself.

Lamont was full of himself—selfish, self-absorbed. Everything was about him. Nicole dumped him after a package arrived at her condo addressed to her from some heffa named Latrice. Nicole opened it and found a pair of Lamont's underpants—"draws," as her nana would say. She didn't even wait for an explanation; she recognized them instantly because she had purchased the boxers for him as a gift and had had them monogrammed with his initials, L.D. He enjoyed boasting that it stood for the length of his manhood. Nicole had soon discovered there was another reason for those initials: Limp Dick. He smoked a lot of weed. When she told Keisha about it, she claimed that "smoking those fuckin' blunts is what got that dick in a coma state."

When Nicole showed him the package from Latrice, he stared at the box and the name of the sender, picked up his draws, packed up his shit, and left.

After that experience, Nicole didn't exactly swear off men, but she vowed to be more selective. If she met someone, fine; if not, that was fine, too. Then she met—well remet, actually—Dr. Alan Lovejoy three years ago at their tenth high school reunion.

∘ ∘ ∘

COMING ALONE *was a mistake,* Nicole thought as she entered the main ballroom of the Bellevue Hotel on Broad Street for her ten-year high school reunion. *I wish I had taken Keisha's advice and ridden along with her,* she said to herself. *At least having someone familiar to walk in with would have made this easier.* In spite of the fact that she looked great and had kept herself up during the last ten years, for some reason, Nicole felt sort of nervous.

Keisha, Freda, Mira, Renee, and Tisha had all graduated together in 1995. (Zenora was two years ahead of them, and Valerie was two years behind them, so they weren't going to this reunion.) TLC's "Creep" boomed from the overhead speakers, and already most of her former classmates were wearing it out on the dance floor. *God, I used to love this song! TLC was my group. The girls and I loved these sistahs. The way they dressed, their songs, style—we tried to emulate them. Their biggest song, "No Scrubs," was our anthem.*

Nicole scanned the room and spotted Freda pressed up against her high school sweetheart, Ben, whom she'd heard was married and already had five kids. He and Freda had broken up after he told her that when they graduated he wanted to get married right away and start a family. That had done it, and Freda was out. She told him marriage had no place in her life for a long time because she had a singing career to get started.

It wasn't such an easy breakup, because those two genuinely loved each other. Nicole remembered Freda crying for weeks afterwards, but she'd said there was no way she would give up or push back her career plans for anyone, even if it meant giving up the man she loved.

So she stepped. But to look at those two on the dance floor, anyone would have thought they were still lovers. Ben was grinding all over her and sweating like a slave.

Where was that man's wife? Even though she was apparently enjoying it, didn't Freda know he was married? But hey, Freda was center stage, which meant she had the attention of most of the onlookers, just like she liked it.

Nicole locked eyes for a quick moment with Joan Wilson, her old high school nemesis, who still looked great. Her svelte figure and toned body almost made Nicole give herself another look. Joan and Nicole were the two most popular girls in high school, and they ran against each other for prom queen, head cheerleader, and class president. Nicole had won all three. They exchanged plastic smiles across the room.

Her rivalry with Joan was a piece of cake compared to the girls she'd had to deal with in middle school—the Brown Sugas.

○ ○ ○

THE BROWN SUGAS were a rough gang of girls who purposely harassed Nicole while passing her in the halls or by booing her at assemblies. They were far from being anything resembling brown sugar, and not one of them was a mental giant in academics or a star player on the school teams. Their thrills and bad reputation came from badgering anyone who wanted to achieve. Nicole happened to be one of their targets. They were as nasty to her as the brothas when they rolled their eyes and sniggered, "She thinks she's cute 'cuz she's light, bright, and almost white."

Sometimes the chiding brought her to tears, but Nicole's parents would say, "Oh, honey, they're just jealous."

"But why?" she'd ask.

"Well, because you *are* beautiful, baby," her father proudly said.

It had all seemed quite dumb to Nicole because all she wanted to do was fit in and be liked. Now and then she heard news about their drama around drugs, jail, and dogs—the two-legged kind. Out of the entire gang, maybe only three actually graduated from high school. The best time of their lives was going to be high school, topped off with prom night. That was probably the only real positive event they would ever know. Everything after that was downhill for them.

The ones who'd dropped out would hang outside the school and linger around the gate. It was easy to read their sad eyes, which said they wanted to be back in school. Even though there were programs permitting them to reenter, it was too late if no one was there to give them the encouragement they needed to get back. One or two would come to the school yard with their babies as if that child was a badge of accomplishment—a trophy to prove they were women.

But like Nicole's nana said, there was more to life than making a baby. Even a bedbug could make a baby; any female could do that. The real reward for a woman was family.

But anyone from the neighborhood could tell you that most of the Brown Sugas ended their teen years with either pregnancy, probation, or both.

It took Nicole a long time to understand where that sort of negativity came from in the black community.

Nicole learned that it wasn't her light skin, keen features, or fashionable clothes that made them cruel. "No, none of that," her grandmother said. "When you don't like yourself, you can't like anybody else." That wise advice, helped steer Nicole away from negative people like the Brown Sugas.

○ ° ○

NICOLE THEN made her way over to the bar and got a light tap on her shoulder. "Nicole 'Pretty Ass' Lawson." She turned only to get a sloppy wet kiss right on her lips. Shocked and shaken, she recognized Bret Scott—or Bad Breath Bret, as he was called in high school. He had the worst breath of anybody she had ever met. Describing the smell was so difficult because Nicole had never smelled anything like that in her life. Keisha used to say it smelled like "cow shit and fried bacon." *Lord, that man has just kissed me in my mouth.* Nicole immediately opened her clutch purse to look for a napkin to wipe her lips, or for a mint, gum, anything. She found Life Savers and offered one to Bret.

"Naw, girl, I'm good. Do I need one? Whatcha tryin' to say? Ha, ha. So, Nicole, how you been?"

"I'm fine, Bret, and you?"

"How do I look, baby girl?" he said as he twirled around so that she could get a full view of his body.

He really doesn't want me to answer that.

"You look good, Bret," she lied. "Tell me, what are you doing with yourself?"

While he told her about his job as a ticket agent at Amtrak's Thirtieth Street Station, Nicole's eyes teared up from the stench coming out of his mouth, which hit her directly in the face.

"I'm in banking," she said, hoping for a small respite.

He cackled, "Yeah, well, maybe I'll come by one day and get me a loan sometime. Haaaa, haaa."

Help! she thought. Just as she was about to pass out from Bret's funk, Nicole spotted Mira walking in with her lover, Jeanette. Nicole admired Mira because she never hid her sexual preference from anyone, and that reunion night was no different. Mira and Jeanette were hand in hand. What might have seemed like a bold move for many was a natural one for Mira.

The DJ played "Who Can I Run To?" by Escape as Keisha arrived. Keisha walked over to join them and she said, "Damn, what's that smell? Y'all smell that?"

"Smell what?" Jeanette asked.

"I don't know—it smells like cow shit and beans," Keisha said.

Nicole playfully slapped Keisha on the arm and reminded her that the smelly formula was cow shit and bacon, not beans. The women all laughed while Bad Breath Bret stood nearby with a confused look on his face.

"Oh, you're right, cow shit and beans was his sister!" Keisha yelled through her laughter.

Garrett Thompson, one of the most likable people in school, walked in with Maxine Thompson, who hadn't gone to their school, but Nicole recognized her from the old neighborhood. Keisha excused herself as he introduced Maxine as his wife and said they'd met at church a few years ago and that they'd been together ever since.

Maxine asked, "So, Nicole, are you married? Do you love the Lord?"

"No and yes," Nicole replied.

Maxine turned from her and asked Mira the same questions. Mira said "Yes," and then introduced Jeanette as her life partner. The look on Maxine's face was one of pure horror. She then reached in her purse for a religious tract.

"God bless you," she said, and then moved on.

Nicole, Mira, and Jeanette glanced at it in unison and then smiled at the topic: ARE YOU GOING TO HEAVEN?

"I guess she wanted to save our souls," said Jeanette.

Keisha returned, and Nicole asked her what made her leave so abruptly.

"Isn't that the cross-eyed girl you were talking about that went to elementary school with you when you lived in South Philly?"

Nicole nodded her head.

"Yeah, that's what I thought. I didn't want to see her. My great-aunt used to say never look a cross-eyed woman in the face—you'll get bad luck. Another thing, never trust a bow-legged woman, 'cuz she'll wrap dem legs around your man's neck, and he'll be gone. Maybe that's how she got that man; I noticed she had a little bow in those legs of hers."

"Those old folktales are so ridiculous and sick," Nicole said, laughing despite herself.

"Well, they are warnings to live by," Keisha said, walking away again.

"Oh, shit—that's my jam. C'mon, baby," Mira said, leading Jeanette to the dance floor as "This Is How We Do It" by Montell Jordan came on.

Standing alone, Nicole told herself, *Quick, think fast, Nicole,* because Bad Breath Bret was lurking and moving closer and closer.

Not recognizing the man facing the bar, Nicole grabbed his hand and pulled him to the dance floor. Anything to evade Bret, who looked perturbed that she didn't wait for his invitation to dance. Nicole was too engrossed in getting away from Bret, so that she didn't look at her partner, who spilled his drink all over himself when she yanked him away from the bar. She glanced up, but didn't recognize him for a moment or two.

It was Alan Lovejoy. She remembered him with a Kid 'n Play haircut in high school. When they were in high school, the girls referred to him as the boy with the good hair, a term Nicole hated. What the hell was *good hair,* anyway? His body was buff beyond belief, not in a grotesque over-sized wrestler-on-steroids way, but like a brotha who took pride in how he looked. And Alan Lovejoy looked good.

"Excuse me. Nicole Lawson?"

"Yes, I'm Nicky. I'm sorry for making you spill that drink. I was trying to get away from someone. Is there anything I can do to take care of that cleaning bill? I'm so sorry." Nicole felt like she was babbling.

He moved the lapel of his jacket to show his name tag, which read, HELLO, MY NAME IS ALAN.

Nicole extended her hand to shake his, but Alan took her by surprise and gave her a big hug. It was sincere, warm, and gentle. She felt a great deal of strength in those arms.

"I think you were trying to escape Bret. Didn't he used to be called Bad Breath Bret?"

And that was how they started their first conversation. Nicole found him so refreshing to talk with. Even though his background was in medicine and hers was investment banking, their conversation was easy and natural.

○ ○ ○

NICOLE CAME BACK to the present and put on Jill Scott's latest CD. She checked her answering machine to discover a message from Valerie apologizing for being late and that she would be there soon. There was also a message from Alan telling her how much he loved her, and that he was jealous he couldn't spend the night with his girl.

Thank goodness for Bad Breath Bret, Nicole thought. He may never realize that he was the one who'd brought her and Alan together.

Nicole used to think it was corny when a woman said, "He completes me," or "He is my soul mate."

But after meeting Alan, she got it. Alan was "the one."

What attracted her to him the most was that he was so unpretentious about his career and his accomplishments. He told her he was following in the footsteps of his parents, who were doctors. His dad was retiring soon, and Alan would take over the practice in Springfield, a suburb of Philadelphia.

A few years ago, his mother was diagnosed with kidney

disease. Alan was a perfect match; therefore, without question or pause, he donated one of his own. Nicole's mother always said, "Yes, you can tell what type of man he is by the way he treats his mother." But Nicole's friends worried that she would fall in the same trap of another "meddling mother" as she'd experienced with Jerry.

But Alan was his own man, and Dr. Lovejoy understood her place with him. Alan made sure that both Nicole and his mother felt like they were the two most important women in his life. Nicole knew that any woman who felt that a man was going to put his lover over his own mother was a damn fool and was just setting herself up for trouble. So when his mother brought over chicken soup when he was sick or looked for that weekly telephone call or visit, Nicole encouraged the attention. She found it sweet and realized that there should never be any competition between her and Dr. Lovejoy, just mature respect. She understood all of this because she could never put any man over her own father. Unlike some women, she could never yield to her husband turning into her father. Not her. She had a father and she had her man—and no one confused the two.

Nicole's parents had been married thirty-six years, and she was sure they had their share of trials and tribulations. What relationship hadn't? She always knew when her mother was peeved with her father for something he did or did not do. Whenever she saw her mother digging or planting in the backyard late at night, she knew Mom was angry about something. Nicole's father would conveniently retire to the den with the TV blasting. Soon after, he'd fall asleep in his La-Z-Boy recliner. That was their way of giving each other space. But in all her thirty-one years, Nicole had never witnessed a cross word between them.

The next morning, after the disagreement, Nicole's mother would go to the den, turn off the TV, and her father would wake up as cheerful as a red robin in spring.

"Barry, you musta been watching something awful good on TV last night for you not to come to bed." Her mother would laugh out loud, and her father would reply, "Not really, apple pie. I was just flipping channels 'n' got comfortable."

"Well, go on in there and get your breakfast and coffee." With a kiss on his forehead, her mother would send him off to the kitchen, and Nicole's father would pick up the morning paper that she had left by the chair. That was Nicole's model for a loving but realistic relationship, and she planned to have the same with Alan.

Six

Do You Think I'm Sexy?

DENISE RUSHED into the police station. She didn't get surprised too often, but this call had been unexpected.

"You are holding a client of mine, and I'd like to see him," Denise told the bored-looking desk sergeant.

"Your client's name?" he asked.

"Kevin Jameron."

"Oh," he said with a smirk.

Denise chose not to ask him why Kevin had been arrested, because the sergeant looked like he'd be only too pleased to tell her, and she wasn't about to give him the satisfaction.

"Hang out here for a moment, and we'll get him out of holding. Someone will escort you into one of the interrogation rooms where you can talk with him."

After a few minutes, Denise was taken to a small room that stank of stale coffee and sweat to wait for her client, Kevin Jameron, who also happened to be Keisha's brother.

For the past three years, Kevin had been the number-one news anchor on the CBS affiliate in Philadelphia, a position he fought long and hard for after graduating from Temple University, where he'd majored in Journalism and Business. After college, he interned at WHYY-TV, the PBS Channel 12 affiliate in Philadelphia, and was asked to co-host several on-air pledge drives. His good looks, charm, and charisma came across so well on screen that pledges routinely jumped whenever he was on. Offers started coming in from New York, Chicago, and Los Angeles, requesting his demo tape. But Philadelphia was where he wanted to remain, so when he was offered the weekend anchor spot for Fox, he jumped at the chance, and his popularity soared. When an anchor position opened at CBS, he didn't have to lobby hard for it, because they wanted him that badly. The city loved him.

When he entered the interrogation room, his rumpled, embarrassed appearance was a far cry from the attractive, confident persona he usually projected.

"Kevin, are you okay?" Denise asked.

"Yes," he said in a monotone.

"Now, before I can get you out of here, I need to know what happened," Denise said.

"Denise, I'm a little embarrassed. Did you tell Keisha you were coming here?"

"No. I haven't had a chance to talk to anyone. I was on

my way to Nicole's bachelorette party when I got your call. So, what's up?"

"Well, before I tell you, you have to promise me that you won't tell my sister—or anyone else. What I tell you stays here. Okay?"

"Kevin, what's going on? What did you do?"

"I guess I better start at the beginning."

○ ○ ○

KEVIN MET OLIVIA CHASE, a stunning thirtyish, five-foot-nine brunette through another anchor friend, Jarvis Mathers. Olivia posed as a socialite and business owner, and at one time she modeled locally, although she'd never really made it past a few successful jobs in New York. Jarvis told Kevin, who had a reputation for sleeping around, that Olivia had some girls if he was interested. Kevin contacted Olivia, met her for lunch, and became a client. Olivia operated her business out of a day spa she owned and operated in Cherry Hill, New Jersey.

During their first meeting, Olivia told Kevin two things: The reason she'd considered bringing him in as a regular client was because Jarvis vouched for him. And anonymity was a must.

She informed him that all appointments would take place in a nondescript building on Admiral Wilson Boulevard, a main thoroughfare leading toward Pennsauken, New Jersey.

"What type of services are you looking for?" Olivia asked.

"You might think I'm sick after I tell you," Kevin said, slightly embarrassed.

Olivia let out a howl. "I assure you that there is nothing that you can say that would shock me," Olivia said.

"Okay, then," Kevin said, taking a big breath. "I'm into S & M and bondage, abuse, both verbal and physical. In other words—the kinkier, the better. I'm looking for a dominatrix who understands my desires. I like to be verbally and physically degraded and humiliated, and I enjoy being tied up and spanked."

"Okay, then, I think I have a few girls who fit the bill," Olivia said, amused by his admission.

After considering various women, Kevin settled on Dahlia, an exotic dark-haired beauty who was one of Olivia's best girls. Since that first meeting, a year ago, Kevin and Dahlia had met more than forty times for their romps in the hay. Kevin could not get enough of Dahlia. Most dominatrices could be very masculine and hard-looking, but Dahlia was the complete opposite. She was sweet, dainty, and very innocent—like a schoolgirl, but she still took on a toughness when in the role of mistress. Last night's session was bittersweet. Dahlia had decided to leave Olivia's business and move to the West Coast to start her own service. It was to be their final session. Kevin paid $2,100 for an overnighter.

When Dahlia stepped out of the shower and entered the room, Kevin was able to catch a glimpse of this beautiful creature. He got an erection just thinking about everything they had done a few hours earlier. They'd tried something new: hypoxyphilia, during which he was deprived of oxygen in order to achieve an orgasm. Dahlia had made Kevin get on his back and then tied his arms and spread his legs. Once he was aroused, she would mount him and tie a clear plastic bag over his head. Kevin chose that dangerous method because the mere fact that it had caused a few accidental deaths excited him even more. As he climaxed, Dahlia ripped off the bag, leaving him gasping for air. The rush satisfied him like nothing else he had ever done.

"You're finally awake, huh?" Dahlia asked.

"Yes, I am. Wow, baby, that was some night. I can't believe you're leaving me. What time is it?"

"Around noon," she replied, then suddenly drew back the curtain, letting in piercing sunlight, which blinded him momentarily.

He pulled the bedsheet over his face to escape the light. "Hey, cut that out."

Dahlia laughed at her prank and closed the drapes. She noticed the twenty-one hundred-dollar bills stacked neatly next to her whip and mask on the bedroom table.

"Why don't you come over here and take care of this for me, Mistress?" Kevin pleaded for one more session as he displayed his stiff manhood.

"I'd love to stay and play, but it is time for me to go," she said, smiling.

"But I haven't received my full twenty-four hours of service, and technically I'm due one more hour." Kevin pleaded in a childlike voice, "Mistress, I'll pay you another five hundred dollars if you spank me with your dog collar. I promise I'll be the best puppy you ever had."

Dahlia pondered a few moments and then decided to oblige.

Kevin became giddy with excitement. "Thank you, Mistress." He got on all fours and allowed her to put the studded dog collar and leash around his neck. Dahlia then told him to sit and be a good boy while she changed into her costume. Kevin couldn't contain his excitement as he sat patiently like a dog waiting for a bone.

His cell phone rang; it was a call from his sister, Keisha. He dared not answer it unless he asked for permission from his mistress. He hollered through the door, asking for her command to get his call. Dahlia gave him permission, but told him he had to make it short.

"Hey, Keisha, what's up?"

"Hey, Kevin, I'm going to have to cancel our dinner date tonight, because I have to pick up Freda from the airport."

"Okay," Kevin said, trying to rush her off the phone.

Keisha sensed he was not alone. "Boy, what are you doing? Where you at?"

Kevin's long pause was explanation enough, as far as she was concerned. She knew he was a slut. "Never mind. Look, call me in the afternoon when you get your nasty ass up." Both brother and sister started laughing.

"Okay, bye," Kevin said before taking his position back on the floor, waiting for his mistress to reenter the room. The anticipation of being dominated by a woman excited

Kevin to no end. Dahlia, now dressed in all-black leather, flung open the door, cracked the whip to get his attention, and then slowly walked toward him, ready to give a command. The anticipation kept him aroused. Anticipation, anticipation.

Suddenly there was a heavy knock on the door. *"Police, open up!"*

Kevin tried to get dressed, and Dahlia scurried to the bathroom for an escape as five federal officers rushed in, guns drawn, and arrested Dahlia and Kevin within seconds. The officers recognized him immediately. One of the officers read them their Miranda rights, but Kevin wasn't listening. All he could think about was the end of his career.

Dahlia didn't go peacefully. She started screaming obscenities and kicking the arresting officers. Someone had tipped the media about the raids, and they were right there to catch all the action when officers made the busts. Aggressive newscasters surrounded them with questions and close shots. A CBS cameraman reluctantly positioned himself for a close shot, because he was not only one of Kevin's coworkers, but a friend. It was a media holiday for the cameras and microphones. Dahlia was still dressed in her black leather costume, while Kevin was in a stupor and wore only silk briefs. A federal officer exited the building behind them, carrying a black leather mask and a black rhinestone studded cat-o'-nine-tails.

On the ride to jail, Kevin was in the backseat of the police car, numb. The feds told him this was one of many arrests as a result of a four-month investigation. They had tapes, photos, and testimony from one of Olivia's girls, who'd tipped them off about the operation. The informer thought she had been treated unfairly by Olivia, who was raking in millions.

○ ○ ○

KEVIN FINISHED telling his story and he finally worked up the courage to look Denise in the eye. While she wanted to drop her jaw to the ground, she didn't wish to add to her client's distress. Denise looked Kevin squarely in the eye and projected the confidence he needed to see in her.

"Kevin, I'll do all I can to get you out of this. It's too late to get you out tonight, and I'll try to do what I can tomorrow, but you know it's Nicole's wedding day and it's the weekend. Just be patient, and I'll get you out as soon as possible."

Kevin knew one thing for sure: He wasn't going to be at Nicole's wedding tomorrow.

Seven

You Wanna Be Startin' Somethin'?

VALERIE HAD settled into Nicole's apartment and was arranging snacks and fruit trays while Nicole got ready for the bachelorette party. The phone rang, and Valerie called out to Nicole, "Nicole, your phone. Nicky?"

The sound of running water indicated that Nicole was still in the shower, so Valerie decided to answer the phone. "Hello? Oh, hi, Tisha, it's Valerie. . . . Nicky's in the shower. . . . You're not? . . . What's the matter? . . . Oh, I see. . . . Okay, well I'll tell her. . . . Can I bring you anything? . . . Okay, sorry. . . . Bye, Tish."

Valerie was puzzled by Tisha's unpleasant tone and the way she cut off the call. She could sense that something was wrong, but Valerie was a little preoccupied with an unsuccessful business meeting she'd had earlier. She was supposed to sign a lease on a new building for her day-care business, but had hit yet another delay. But she'd vowed not to let it get her down and ruin everyone else's evening and instead chose to focus on the gladiolas and calla lilies perfectly arranged in a Waterford crystal vase Nicole had received at one of her wedding showers. Hopefully their beauty, class, and simple elegance would set the tone for the evening.

Making her way over to the sofa, Valerie picked up a photo album that had been neatly placed on a stack of magazines under the coffee table. Flipping through it, she recognized many of the old family and school photos of all the girls throughout the years of their friendship. She came across one that made her laugh out loud.

Just then, Nicole entered in a robe, holding a glass of her favorite white wine, looking for something. "Have you seen my nail polish?"

Valerie was immersed in the photo album and didn't hear her.

"Valerie Coates, I thought you were here to help me get things set up. You're taking a break already?"

"I'm sorry, Nicky. I was just looking at some of our old photos. I can't believe you still have all these."

Nicole sat down next to Valerie and spotted a photo taken of all the girls at Hershey Amusement Park when they were about fourteen years old.

"Jesus, this one is funny. Look at all of us. And oh, my God, the hair! Will you look at our hairstyles! Look at Keisha. Hey, remember how we all laughed because her brother hid her shoes and she had to wear sneakers with her outfit?"

"Girl, we were so fly."

"Yes, we were, but I also remember that Keisha was so mad. Look at her face. And would you look at Denise? Even then she looked like she was in charge of everything."

"When does Denise Upshaw listen to anyone but Denise Upshaw? When she found out that Alan and I were getting married and that we wanted to keep everything low-key—no big wedding, no fanfare—she had a fit."

In a mocking voice, Valerie imitated Denise: "Absolutely not, Nicole Lawson. We *will* be having a party for your closest friends. I *will* take care of everything. Now that's final, end of discussion." Valerie fell back on the sofa laughing as Nicole joined in.

"You sound just like her!"

"Please don't tell her. She'll get mad at me. Promise me."

"Girl, don't worry about Denise. She's more bark than bite. And besides, it is just a joke. You know what? I think you should do your impersonation of her tonight while everyone is here."

"Are you crazy? She would never speak to me again, and you know that! She still hasn't spoken to Zenora since she claimed Z messed up her hair on purpose when *Essence* magazine did the photo shoot with her for their 'Woman on the Move' section. I actually thought it looked nice."

"It did look nice. There are a lot of things one could say about Zenora, but when it comes to hair, we all know she's the best. Denise just got angry because she was not in control of where she was placed in the photo, and she felt it was because the talent coordinator was not feeling her hairstyle. He placed her in the back. She let her ego get in the way."

"She means well. I just don't want to get on her wrong side."

"You are so sweet. Girl, who could be mad at you?"

"Denise!" Valerie assured.

"Just like in school everybody loved you. You were the only girl that didn't have *one* girl jealous or mad at you. You're still sweet, kind, and one of my dearest friends."

Valerie gave Nicole a hug. "Thanks, Nicky."

"No, I mean it. I love all you girls, but you're the only one that never had any drama. You will make some guy very lucky one day, that's for sure."

"You think so?"

"I know so. You just have to open up a little bit more. You're too shy around guys."

"I am *not*!"

"Okay, here's an example: Remember when we had Keisha's birthday party a couple of years ago at the Pyramid Club here in town, and Rick Fox, the basketball player, was there? He asked you to dance, you said you couldn't and excused yourself to go to the restroom. Girl, you didn't come out for thirty minutes."

"That is not true! If I remember correctly, I had a really bad stomachache—and besides, he was married," Valerie said as she walked to the bar area and got a bottle of spring water.

Nicole teased, "He was *separated* and had filed for divorce. Everybody knew it. And every single girl was on him except you. If I remember correctly, he came over to you. Besides, what's wrong with just an innocent dance?"

Valerie stuttered, "Well, I—I couldn't. I like Vanessa Williams."

"You don't even know Vanessa Williams!"

"So, it doesn't matter. It just didn't seem right. As a matter of fact, I don't think he should have been in the club. Technically he was *not* single. And what was he doing in Philly anyway?"

"Wasn't that the NBA All-Star Game weekend?"

"Oh, that's right," Valerie remembered.

"It was public knowledge that those two were having problems. Listen, he asked you to dance, not go back to his hotel room with him. He is fine, though."

"I'm not really into those high-profile guys. They get spoiled with all that attention. When I do settle down, it's going to be with someone that is not in the public eye, and is very much single. And why are we talking about this right now, anyway? Aren't you supposed to be getting ready for your party, miss?"

Nicole took another sip of wine before getting up. "Okay, whatever. Let me get dressed. You're just trying to change the subject. Didn't I hear the phone ring?"

"Sorry, it was Tisha. She's not going to make it tonight."

"What! Why not?" Upset, Nicole sat back down on the sofa.

"She's not feeling well. I asked her if there was anything that any of us could do, and she snapped at me. She really didn't sound good at all."

"That's a bummer. This might be the last time we may all be able to chill together for a while. Was it one of her migraines?"

"I don't know. She was very vague. It was a short conversation. In fact, she cut me off, but she said to tell everyone she was sorry."

"I hope she's okay."

"You know, ever since Kimmy was born, Tisha's been getting these migraines off and on, and she won't see a doctor," Nicole said, her brow wrinkled with concern. "I've asked her time and time again to see a doctor, but she won't do it. Do you think she and Roland had another argument? Maybe she's just using not feeling well as an excuse."

"I don't know. I just try to stay out of their marriage. Tisha has made it quite clear that the topic is off-limits."

"I'm just saying, it's a possibility. He's always nice around us—most of the time, anyway—but I've called the house a number of times, and there he is in the background, screaming. When I ask her what's up, she says he was just upset about something at work. But you're right, you can't intervene in grown folks' business when you're really not sure what's going on."

At that moment, Nicole's intercom system buzzed. It was the front-desk clerk letting her know she had visitors. Nicole jumped up and started back to her bedroom.

"It's time. The gang is beginning to arrive, so let me get dressed. Do me a favor, Val? Do *not* let Freda or Keisha in my bedroom. Every time one of those hoochies comes in my room, they leave with an outfit. Especially Freda."

"No, they don't." Val started laughing as she pushed Nicole toward her bedroom. The bell outside the apartment chimed, letting Valerie know someone was at the door.

"Coming!" Val shouted out.

○ ○ ○

ON THE OTHER SIDE of the door stood Freda and Keisha. As they waited for the apartment door to open, Freda said, "Now, Keisha, don't start no shit with this girl tonight."

"Girl, what are you talking about?"

"Bitch, don't play with me. You know what I'm talking about. Don't start in with your teasing and shit on Val. Nicky called me earlier to say Val's closing didn't go through today."

"Aww, shit—what happened?"

Just then, Valerie opened the door and greeted both of them with hugs. "Hey, Freda. Hey, Keisha."

"Where's Nicole?" Keisha shouted.

Freda looked toward the bedroom and yelled, "Come on, girl! It's time to get the party started."

Keisha made her way to Nicole's latest editions of fashion magazines. After picking through them, she settled instead on reading her own selection of gossip rags, which were her full-time entertainment. She stretched away from the magazine to grab a handful of chips and parked in a comfortable spot on the sofa.

"I can't believe it," she blared out.

"Believe what?" Valerie took a look over Keisha's shoulder to see what the excitement was all about.

"Oprah is pregnant, chile!" Keisha exclaimed.

"Really? Is she showing?" Valerie strained her neck, trying to spot photos on the pages of a pregnant Oprah.

"Now, you know Keisha believes everything in those tabloids," Freda said.

"It says it right here, in big bold black letters." Keisha pointed to the headline. STEADMAN *MAD*! BECOMES *DAD* WITH PURSE-HOLDER OPRAH WINFREY!

"Wait, Keisha. Isn't she a little beyond her child-bearing years?"

Freda answered, "Fifty-four, no more eggs."

Keisha responded, "That means absolutely nothing when you have that much money. They can create you some more eggs. Says right here that gal pal Gayle is furious because she's the one that wanted more kids."

Freda eased her way down the hallway toward the bedroom. "Where's Nicole? Nicky, Ms. Freda's here, girl. Where you at?"

"Yeah, I want to see her, too," said Keisha as she got up to join her.

Valerie quickly intercepted Keisha and Freda and nervously motioned for them to stop. "Uhmm, Nicky told me not to let either one of you in her room."

"Why?" Freda asked.

"That's what I wanna know," Keisha chimed in with hands on her hips, giving Valerie a hard look.

"Because—ah—ah—because she doesn't want anyone to see her outfit before she comes out. Yeah, that's it."

Rolling her eyes, Freda threw a nasty look to Keisha. "Oh, okay, it's like that, huh? She thinks I want to borrow something. Well, she's wrong—I don't. Besides, Nicky's shit ain't all that. I was just gonna holla at her, that's all. Let me go over here and get my ass a drink. You want something Keisha?"

"Girl, you know I start the evening off with a Heineken. Make sure it's cold. I don't play that room-temperature shit. That's that white-people shit. If it ain't cold, I don't want one. And speaking of her clothes, she did have on a bad business suit the other day when I stopped by the bank to see her. I was like, 'Girl, I don't borrow nobody's shit, but that suit was tight!'"

Freda passed Keisha a Heineken and joined her on the sofa.

Before accepting it, Keisha touched the bottle with her hand to test its temperature. "It'll do. Thanks, girl," Keisha said before she raised the bottle, toasting Freda.

"I like all of Nicole's clothes. She has always had good taste." Val smiled.

"Please, like I said, she do a'ight." Freda added, flipping through the photo album that Valerie and Nicole were looking through earlier.

"You look nice, Freda," Valerie offered.

"Thanks, girl. But when don't I look nice? Let me go on and step this off for y'all."

Freda began to model her outfit as if she were on an haute couture runway. "Got it at Bloomingdale's King of Prussia Mall—skirt a hundred and seventy dollars, pumps two eighty-five, blouse—"

Nicole entered the room and interrupted: "Blouse, mine!"

Caught by surprise, Freda tried to play it off. "Oh, girl, this is yours? When did you give this to me? I mean *lend* it to me?"

"I didn't. You lifted it when you left here last week."

"I know you ain't tryin' to say I stole your blouse, 'cuz I will take this off right now. I just didn't remember, that's all." Freda started to unbutton the blouse.

Nicole gave her a stern look because she knew Freda was bluffing, causing Keisha to burst into a laugh.

"Bitch, I don't believe you're going to let me stand here and take this blouse off, forcing me to go back to your closet and find me another one that matches my damn skirt."

They all laughed.

Nicole put her arm around Freda. "Girl, I'm not mad at you. It's just sometimes I'll go to my closet to put on a particular article of clothing only to find it's not there. Then that's when I know either you or Keisha was the culprit."

Keisha added in her two cents: "Yeah, bitch, you do be stealing."

Nicole continued her playful warning. "And another thing, you've tried that same tired stunt before—threatening to take off something. So save it. It looks good on you. Just keep it. Besides it was a gift from someone—I can't remember who—and I never really cared for it. It really isn't my style. It's nice and expensive, but it's more you than me, Freda, so please keep it."

Freda rolled her eyes. "Well, I'm not so sure I want it now. I mean, you putting my ass on front street ain't cool. I just didn't remember that it was yours."

"Keep it!" Nicole demanded.

"Well, since you insist, I will. Thanks, girl." She hugged Nicole.

"You're welcome. But why are you so dolled up? It's just us girls tonight."

Just as Freda was about to answer, Keisha interrupted with another announcement from the headlines of the tabloid.

"Now you know that this makes no sense! J. Lo is getting an ass reduction. Would you look at this picture?" She tried to show the article to Nicole and Freda, who ignored her. Valerie was the only one who rushed over to get a look.

"Put that shit down. In fact, I've got some good news," Freda said. "I had an audition earlier today."

That drew everyone's attention, but Keisha still had one eye on her J. Lo article.

"You know the seventies singer Freda Payne, my mom's old friend from her club days?"

"Freda Payne. 'Band of Gold,' right?" Nicole remembered. "Wow, I haven't heard that name or song in a long time. That's a classic oldie. We used to karaoke that one to death. Is she still performing?"

Keisha broke in, "Hell yeah, that diva is still singing, and she can rag her ass off. I saw her on TV for a Quincy Jones tribute honoring his life. You know they used to go together. Well, anyway, Nancy Wilson and Chaka Khan were on the show, too. They looked nice, but when the camera panned across the room and focused on Freda, I was like, Who is this bitch looking this damn good? Then the name flashed up on the screen: Freda Payne. The bitch is class personified!"

"You do not have to say *bitch*. And why must you always curse? It's not necessary," Valerie said.

"Ah, bitch, shut up!" Keisha said as she rolled her eyes. "It's just a figure of speech, and you know I talk like that. Anyway, in his autobiography, he told the story of how they hooked up."

"Can I finish my damn story?" Freda said impatiently. "It's not all about those damn celebrities and stars you're reading about. I'm trying to share some shit about my career with y'all. Damn! Is it possible that I have a moment?"

"Girl, go 'head and tell us your story," Keisha said as she got up and went to the bar for another beer.

"Anyway, there's a European tour of the legendary female singers of the 1970s and 1980s, and her people were holding auditions for two backup singers. I really want this job because she is going to let each girl perform a solo number while she changes outfits. It's a seventeen-city tour beginning in two weeks."

"That's great, Freda," Valerie said. "You know you already got it. You can sing, you're stunning, and you were even named after her, right? Come on, you're in."

"I don't know. The audition was really hard. She performs all genres of music, and in her show there's jazz, pop, R and B, and Broadway. People think that just because you haven't seen a particular artist in quite some time or they don't have a record on the top of the charts that they're sitting in some small run-down apartment crying broke. But Europe is where a lot of artists go and have lucrative careers way after the hits have stopped."

Keisha interrupted. "Look, if she was really cool, she'd just give you the spot. Audition for what? She does know you can sing, right?"

"Yes, but it doesn't work that way. Besides, I don't want it to be given to me just because she knew my mom. I want it because I was the best bitch that walked up to the mic. You feel me? As a matter of fact, I didn't even bring up who I was until after the audition was over and I got a call-back notice. She was shocked because she hadn't seen me since I was a little girl. She said she reached out to my mom several times, but hadn't heard back from her."

"Where was the audition?" Valerie asked.

"The Apollo Theater in Harlem. We had to be there at nine a.m. last Monday for an open call. Usually I don't do open calls, because they're like a cattle call—everyone and their momma standing in line and some that shouldn't be because they can't sing. It was long and tedious, but I made it through. But you know what was wonderful? Having the opportunity to perform on that legendary stage and then walking through the building glancing at all the photos of all the singing artists adorning the walls. I did my best at my callback audition this morning, and I'm one step closer to getting the spot. I'm just going to claim it, plain and simple."

"That's the attitude, Freda. Not the bitch part, but good for you," Valerie said.

Taking a swig of her beer, Keisha added, "Yeah, right.

Listen, in that business, it's who you know, and stars do favors for friends all the time. I would have told her by the
time I got there who I was. Shit! I would've made that bitch
remember my name. Why don't your mom and her talk
anymore?"

"Who knows? I'm not in contact with my family much,
you guys know that. And with my mom being so heavily
committed to the church, I'm sure that she doesn't want to
talk to Freda Payne. It reminds her too much of the past."

"Girl, your momma still one of those Witnesses?"
Keisha asked.

"Keisha! That's rude," Valerie said.

"What's rude about it? I just asked was she still one of
Jehovah's Witnesses."

"Yes, she is," Freda said matter-of-factly.

"I'm not saying this about your momma, but they asses
can be annoying. I remember on Saturday mornings when
I was growing up, they'd be on their street patrol. When
they came up on our porch, my grandmother would close
the blinds, turn off the TV, and make us be quiet. They
knew we were home because they would actually see the
blinds closing. But that didn't stop them, because like
clockwork they returned week after week until one day
when my grandmother just got fed up. She opened the
door, stood on the porch, and waited for them. They
greeted her with a smile and said, 'Good morning, sister,
how are you today? Would you like to know about Jehovah?' And my grandmother said, 'First of all, all my sisters
are dead; second, it's not such a good morning because I

didn't hit the number; and third, I don't wanna know no Jehovah! I'm a United Methodist, and I know Jesus—so get off my porch and don't come back here no more.' "

Everyone laughed.

"And as for stars doing favors for friends, Keisha, if that's the case, how come your brother didn't just hook me up when Channel Ten held its first annual Sing-Off on the Air Concert Series?"

"You won the damn contest, didn't you?" Keisha remarked.

"Yes. After standing in line for over three and a half hours and being number 155 in line. But I didn't mind it, and I won fair and square."

"That's the way to do it, girl," Nicole said.

"That's how playas do it, baby. I knew I had to bring it because most of those girls in line were at least a decade younger than me."

"My brother is the anchor, not the producer at the station," Keisha said. "He does not book talent. Seriously, how would that look?"

Valerie and Freda stared at Keisha, who backed down after realizing that what she'd just said conflicted with her previous argument. "Okay, fine—I get it."

"How is Kevin, Keisha? I saw him on the air the other night. Is he losing weight?" Nicole asked.

Although she'd never told Keisha, Kevin was Nicole's first. Nicole was sixteen, Kevin was eighteen, and it just happened. They were both junior camp counselors at a summer Christian camp in the Pocono Mountains. They were there for three weeks and had a little adventure of their own. Nicole had always had a crush on Kevin, so giving in to his advances was not that difficult. He never looked at her the same after that, and they were both surprised that they had gone as far as they had. Their friendship became more like a brother–sister thing after that night. Nicole never regretted it, because that's when she became a woman.

"You know my brother thinks he's the finest brotha in Philly. He's at Gold's Gym twenty-four–seven. I told him he should just take some of his money and invest it into his own gym. Actually, I spoke with him earlier today. I had to cancel our dinner so that I could meet up with Freda on time."

While Freda made her way to the snack table, she remarked, "Yeah, but I see your brother with too many sistahs! When a brotha is that good-looking, and he ain't married yet, he's screwing *any-* and *every*thing but a goldfish!"

Keisha and Nicole laughed.

"Freda!" Valerie said in an embarrassed tone.

But Freda continued, "Oh, excuse me—everybody but Valerie, who at twenty-eight is still a virgin."

They locked eyes, and Valerie reminded her that her sex life was none of her business.

"That's true, girl, because I don't know how you do it or, should I say, don't do it. Because I have *needs*. At least three or four times a week. Needs, bitch! Needs!" Keisha yelled dramatically.

Valerie excused herself and disappeared into Nicole's bedroom. Usually she could tolerate Freda and Keisha's badgering—but not today—not with all she'd been through before arriving at the party.

Nicole said to the others, "Valerie will be okay. You know how embarrassed she gets about personal stuff like that. I thought I told you to lay off that teasing today. She's had a big disappointment and is not taking it too well."

Without remorse, Keisha remarked, "Why? Shit, she should be embarrassed. Twenty-eight years old and the only dick she sees is when she walks that ol' mangy dog of hers."

Eight

I Sing Because I'm Happy; I Sing Because I'm Free

"SPEAKING OF DICK, I know there has got to be a few honeys coming by this piece tonight, 'cuz Ms. Freda is ready for a little fun," Keisha said as she and Freda looked at Nicole.

"Don't ask me. Denise and you guys were in charge of this night. But let's make one thing clear: *I don't need any strippers.* So if you guys have any of this happening, remember—it's for you, not for me, because I have Alan."

Keisha started gagging.

"Ooh, girl, you all right? What's the matter?" Nicole asked, concerned.

"Excuse me, I just threw up in my mouth," Keisha said, and Freda broke out laughing.

"That's cold—you know that's cold, girl," Nicole said, playfully slapping Keisha on the arm.

"Alan is all right. I mean, I like the brotha, but he's a little on the corny side," Keisha said.

Freda teased, "You didn't think that when y'all dated."

"Thank you!" Nicole slapped five with Freda.

"Okay, bitches, we were ten! The closest we ever came to any kind of contact was when I made him share his last Lemonhead candy with me. He bit it off and gave me half. Like I said, he's all right, but he ain't never been a snack that Ms. Keisha wanted to nibble on."

"I gotta agree with my girl here. Alan's cute, cool, and he's a doctor, but a little too straitlaced for my taste. I like a brotha with a little more edge. You know, like T.I. or Fiddy," added Freda.

"Well we all know *that,* Ms. Freda. If he ain't been on lockdown at least once in his life, you don't want him," Nicole said as she and Keisha giggled.

"Now, wait a minute. Randall ain't never been on lockdown," Freda said of her latest love interest.

"No, 'cuz they ain't caught his ass yet! I done told you, girl—leave that rough trade alone. None of them are worth anything but a fuck, and that's it," Keisha said.

"Well, sometimes that's all I want. Thank you very much." Freda rolled her eyes.

"Dr. Alan Lovejoy . . . that's my man, y'all. I have never had a brotha treat me as good as Alan treats me. The surprising thing is no one would have ever thought that he and I would hook up after all these years. Ladies, I have hit the jackpot. He is kind, considerate, loving, supportive, and—"

"—Corny," interrupted Keisha.

"And you know what? You're right. He is corny, but I like his corniness. I love the fact that he really thinks his jokes are funny even though nobody laughs but me, or when we go dancing and he thinks he's Usher, but moves more like Kid Rock. He's just being himself, and I love that. So I'll laugh at the corny jokes and dance with Kid Rock. It's all good because I know he loves me. I am his princess, and he definitely is my prince."

Silence.

Keisha returned to the bar for another drink and broke the quiet in the room.

"Will somebody put this bitch on Lifetime TV for Women so some of those lonely bitches who need to hear a sappy story can hear hers, 'cuz I don't want to! Now, shit, I'm over here for a good time, and I want to see some eight-packs, bubble asses, and swivel sticks in my face. I want it to be HBO after midnight up in here, not no doggone Bobby Jones Gospel on Sunday. Now, hell, who hired the snacks for the night?"

"Zenora," Freda responded.

Keisha and Nicole looked at each other, and then responded in unison, "Zenora?"

"Aw, hell naw. It's gonna be like a Spanish fiesta up in here," warned Keisha.

At that very moment, the door opened, and Denise entered. After swiftly walking across the room, she put her bags down and rushed toward the bathroom, but not before addressing each girl with a flip snide remark. No one moved. They all appeared to be stunned.

"Hello, all. I'm sorry I'm late. There was so much to do before I got here."

Passing Keisha, she snatched the tabloid out of her hand. "You know you really need to stop!"

She noticed the blouse that Freda was wearing was a birthday gift she had given Nicole.

"Hmmm, nice blouse, Freda." She then turned to Nicole and said, "If you didn't like your birthday gift, honey, I would have easily exchanged it."

"Girl, did Denise give you that blouse?" Keisha instigated, and Nicole interrupted with a more important matter.

"Forget that. I want to know how Denise got a key to my condo."

Freda was pissed and went back to the blouse issue. "Had I known she gave you this damn blouse, I would have never taken it—I mean borrowed it. Nicole, I'm going home to change. I will not have Denise ragging on me all night about this blouse."

Nicole restrained Freda from leaving and said, "No, you're not going anywhere. Pay her no mind. Denise is just being Denise."

"And she's going to be worse now more than ever," added Keisha, "with the election a few months away and her caseload. I'm surprised she had time even to throw this little get-together for Nicky."

"Look, this party was not my idea," Nicole said. "I told her it was not necessary, but you know Denise."

"To be honest, I have no idea why she would want to leave her successful law practice and enter dirty-ass politics," Freda remarked as she made her way to the dining room table to grab a snack.

"Ha! Like lawyers aren't dirty," Keisha said.

"Keisha!" Nicole warned.

"I'm just saying, what's more crooked than some of these lawyers? Granted, I'm not referring to Denise. Although she *can* be a drama queen, and there are times I can't stand her ass, but, I think my girl's one of the honest ones," Keisha said, unaware that Denise had reentered the room.

"My, my. Keisha Jameron defending my honor." Denise smirked. "Well, sort of . . . What is the world coming to? Frankly, my sisters, you know I've always been one who bores easily with my own success. I'm always reaching for that next level of perfection." Denise took a drink from the bar before continuing "Law is just the beginning. There was a time when all I had my sights set on was a judgeship. However, the mere thought of wearing the same black gown all day, every day, petrified me."

"There she goes, blowing her own horn again," Keisha mumbled under her breath.

"Seriously, though, girlfriends—becoming councilwoman will allow me to have a lot of say in our local politics here in Philly. And I will still be able to keep my practice, at least until I run for mayor."

"Girl, get real! These white folks are not going to allow that!" Freda shouted.

"Really? You'd like to become mayor one day?" Nicole asked while rolling her eyes at Freda.

"President, actually, Nicky. But I'm patient." Denise turned toward Freda. "And, white people will not be the determining factor if a minority female is ever elected as Mayor of Philadelphia. The Latino vote is the key to any hopeful candidate. Just check out all those Puerto Ricans in North Philly. And besides, some of your *cousins* still refuse to vote."

"I don't vote," Freda said somewhat defensively.

"Precisely, Freda, which is why you *will* register for this next election, even if I have to drag you to voter registration myself, and you can work with me at my headquarters. Once my campaign office opens, I'll need all of you to stuff envelopes, make phone calls—all of that volunteer groundwork that wins elections. Now, where is everybody?"

Keisha turned around on the sofa to look at Denise. "Denise, ol' pal, did I hear you say we would be working as volunteers?"

"Of course. I don't have big money coming from the political parties. I've got to do this mostly on my own. That's where my friends can help. But first you've got to register to vote."

"I've been hearing from the bank execs that the incumbent is practically a shoo-in for the primary," Nicole said. "But I'm going to give you all my support. Yes, and even volunteer. Right, Freda?"

"Okay, I'm volunteering if everybody else does, but you better put some fine-looking volunteers in that office working with me. I've got to get paid somehow, if you know what I mean."

"Oh, Freda, must your mind always be on *that*?" Valerie questioned in disgust.

"Like what, Valerie? See, I bet you can't even say it: sex, dick, sex, dick, sex, dick."

Valerie threw her hands up to her ears, tired of Freda's cursing and teasing.

Seeing Valerie's distress, Nicole changed the subject back to Denise's campaign. "Well, you know you have my support both financially and otherwise. I can give you a few hours of office time when Alan and I return from our honeymoon. I can't speak for Zenora, but I'm sure you can put her down for funding and volunteer office time. Now you know one of her shops is in your district, so she might call in a favor when you win this election."

Reluctantly Keisha chimed in, "I'll help, but I ain't working with no ugly men. Put some of those good-looking law clerks up in there, so I can show them what justice is all about—yeah, *just-us*. Ouch!"

All Denise could do was shake her head.

Keisha continued, "Yeah, Freda—you can get a few of your men who wear those ankle bracelets to do something, 'cuz you know they ain't working."

"Watch it," Freda warned.

"Where is everybody?" Denise asked. "I know Renee is running late from her taping at the studio because I spoke with her on the phone. She's taking the Metroliner from Penn Station and arriving at Thirtieth Street Station in about an hour from now."

Valerie responded, "Well, Mira is having water-pipe problems at the club, but she promised to be here. Zenora was called to do some celebrity's hair in Center City. She called to say she'll be late, too, and Tisha can't make it."

At that moment Denise stood and caught a glimpse of herself in the wall mirror hanging above the sofa. She concluded that her lateness had been justifiable and fashionable; theirs was rude and ghetto.

Nicole changed the subject. "Denise, how did you get a key to my place?"

Keisha, still buried in yet another tabloid magazine, added, "Denise probably has one to the White House."

"Not yet, darling, but in due time." Denise winked and smiled at Keisha.

"I'm still waiting for an answer," Nicole said.

By that point, Denise had made her way back to the bar for a refresher. Before dropping each ice cube slowly in her glass, she wondered if it was Tiffany or Waterford crystal she was drinking from. "Nicole Yvette Lawson!" she said, punctuating each of Nicole's names with another ice cube.

"Oh, shit, girl—she said your whole name." Freda laughed.

"Now, you know that we agreed two years ago, after you had your last attack, that I should have a key to your place. Remember how you couldn't get to a phone? It's a good thing your housekeeper was here."

"Yeah, I remember that shit," Freda said. "Girl, you had us all scared."

"Exactly, so I have a key. In fact, I have one for Valerie, Keisha, Zenora—"

Freda murmured, "She ain't got a key to my place, because I don't play that."

"True, Freda, true. I don't. Could it be because you always have to move?" Denise said sarcastically.

Keisha couldn't resist the opportunity to fan the flame."Oh, shit—no, she didn't!"

"Skank!" Freda said, rolling her eyes.

A smiling Denise threw it back to her. "Love you, too."

"Okay, you two," Nicole said. "Come on, now. Stop! You're right, Denise, I forgot about that."

Denise went to retrieve the key from her purse and said, "Now, if you want it back, I will just give it—"

Nicole stopped her. "—Of course not. Please keep the key. And Freda, I know you guys were all scared. I was, too. Diabetes is no joke. It taught me a valuable lesson, though. I will never let my work schedule prevent me from eating or taking my medicine on time. I've been dealing with this disease since I was born. I should have known better. Anxiety and stress will set it off every time."

Denise added, "Nothing is more important than one's health."

"You got that right. Girls, we are no longer twenty-one. Exercise, diet, and living a stress-free life is my goal from now on," said Keisha, who munched on another handful of potato chips while reaching for her third cold beer.

Freda chimed in. "Shit! I'm doing exactly what sistah Jill Scott sang about. 'Living my life like it's golden.' "

All the girls joined in and sang a few bars with her.

"I ain't got time to let too much shit get to me. That's

why I'm going all-out on this singing thing. Tomorrow is not promised. Hell, I'm thirty," Freda said.

"*Whaaat?*" Keisha said in mock shock. But her attempt at a joke fell flat, and Freda became defensive.

"Bitch! Don't try it. We were all in school together. Yo' ass will be thirty in a few weeks, too."

Everyone laughed, including Keisha, who grabbed the TV remote control and pointed it at Freda. "Okay, hold up—I'm gonna need you to turn that shit down." She pressed the button on the remote.

Freda ignored her and kept talking, "Seriously, though, I'm—"

Keisha picked up the remote again and, with a straight face, remarked, "No, bitch! I muted you. What? There's no batteries in this thing?" She tapped the remote as everyone laughed.

When the laughter died down a bit, Freda turned serious. "I'm smart enough to know that my landing a solo record deal is slim. Even though I'm not into old-school music, this Freda Payne opportunity will be good for me. European audiences are so different when it comes to artists—they're more loyal. They get behind them, and they become fans for life. No one cares about the age thing. Black female singers work all the time over there."

Her focus went to the wall mirror, where she saw tears in her eyes. "Who knows, maybe some rich European man will snatch me right up and I really will be living my life like it's golden."

Nicole went over to Freda and held her hands in hers.

"You have charisma, and you can sing your ass off. Look at you—five or ten years can be knocked off your true age. It just hasn't been your time yet, sweetie. This just might be it. I hope so. We all do. We have your back—right, ladies?"

Keisha responded, "Hell yeah," while Denise nodded in agreement.

Still sounding a little insecure, Freda said softly, "I know, but sometimes I get a little scared. I mean, what if I don't really make it? What if I've peaked? I don't even know what else I'd do. It just seems that everyone else is getting their turn but me."

"I'll tell you what you'll do. You'll use that business degree from Hampton and get your ass a job," Denise sternly remarked.

"Ugh! Nine to five scares me, I just can't."

"Bitch, you working nine to five now! Maybe not every day—but you are working nine to five," Keisha said.

Nicole reassured her. "But she won't be for long. Stay positive, Freda. Go in there and do your thing. Claim what's yours. You got this. Now, come on—where's my Freda? Where's that confident sistah that has it all together?"

As she hugged Nicole, Freda smiled. "Thanks, girl. *You've* always had my back." She rolled her eyes at Denise.

"What? *We've* had your back, too. How many times have you performed at one of these tired-ass Philly clubs and I made sure my firm purchased a block of tickets to see you do your thing?" Denise said.

Keisha added, "Thank you. And I know you ain't trying to say that I don't have your back. I promote your ass everywhere I go. Shit! Beyoncé and Ashanti ain't got nothin' on you."

Everyone looked at one another and remarked in surprised unison: *"Ashanti?"*

"My bad. Okay, Beyoncé and Alicia?"

"That's better," Freda said. "Ashanti is cute and she can carry a tune, but let's stay real. I'm in a whole different league. But whatever or however, she got there, and that's where I want to be."

Nine

Get Here if You Can

VALERIE RETURNED to the living room, and Keisha teased, "Girl, I forgot you were even here. What were you doing back there all that time? Playing with yourself?"

"No. For your information, I was trying to reach Tisha on the phone, seeing if she's okay."

"Tisha? What's wrong with her?" Denise asked.

"We're not quite sure. She called earlier and said she wasn't feeling well. She didn't think she was going to make it tonight. I think it's one of her migraines."

Denise was annoyed. "We were *all* supposed to be here."

Nicole said, "Denise, would you relax? Everyone will be here. Actually, I forgot that today was Renee's last day of filming on *Tomorrow Will Come*. No telling how long it took to tape the last scene for the week."

Freda laughed and remarked, "*Tomorrow Will Come,*
that's a dumb-ass name for a soap opera. I don't watch the
show anyway, but why is she the only black chick on there
and playing someone who wants to pass for white?"

"That's the name, Freda. And it's just a character. It's
not really Renee," Nicole said.

"And where's Mira?" Denise asked.

"Mira is still waiting at the club while the broken water
main is being repaired. She and Jeanette had a few other
things that came up at the club as well," Valerie said.

The mere mention of Mira's lover brought a frown to
Freda's face. "Is she bringing her? It's supposed to be
Dickville tonight, not Dykeville."

Keisha guffawed, but Nicole became angry. "Now,
that's enough Freda! Who Mira chooses to be with is her
business. And Jeanette is who she chose. Let it be. She's
been our friend since all of us were in school, and we all
knew then that Mira was a lesbian. We love her, so respect-
ing her lifestyle is not even an option—we just *do.*"

Feeling a little guilty, Freda responded, "Girl, I'm just
playing. You know I love that girl. It's just—I don't get it.
Besides, it's nasty!"

Valerie and Denise shook their heads at Freda.

Nicole continued, "That's just it—it's not for any of us
to get. We're not gay. We *don't have* to get it." Nicole got
up and went into the kitchen.

"Well, it's strictly dickly here. I'm just goin' to put that
out there," Keisha added while waving her hand at everyone.

"I say, to each his own," Denise said, "or is it *her* own? Personally, there's nothing another woman can do for me except my hair, my nails, and if she's got a rich brother, introduce him to me."

Valerie said, "I like Jeanette. She's really cool. We take a Pilates class together, and there's never any talk about sexual preferences. And even if there were, it's just two friends discussing life. And to me, that's very normal."

The telephone rang, and Keisha answered. "It's the front desk. Zenora and Mira are coming up."

Valerie opened the door, and Zenora entered carrying an elaborately wrapped gift, while Mira brought a chilled magnum of champagne.

"Hey, everyone," Mira said, her upbeat attitude not showing any stress from the mishap at her club.

"Hey, y'all. Sorry I'm late," Zenora said. "For a minute there, I wasn't sure I was going to make it. I got an emergency call from the actress Vanessa Bell Calloway, who was supposed to come to the salon, but was stuck at her hotel waiting for her agent to arrive. That meant I had to go to her hotel suite, ASAP, where I gave her a primo style and did her makeup. You know those celeb sistahs can be very demanding."

"Yeah, but it's those emergency calls that bring in the big bucks and helped you with the seed money for your salon," Valerie said.

"True, true," Zenora said as she put down her stuff. "I'm grateful for the clientele, but with high-end clients, sometimes you got to be ready for anything."

"And just so you know, you both have been drafted to help with Denise's campaign. We all have been," Freda announced to Zenora and Mira.

"Oh, that's fine with me," Zenora said. "Denise, count me in on distributing flyers, stickers, placards—anything you need. One of my salons is in your district, so of course I'm going to help. I got some neighborhood kids who can also do a good job for you."

"Zenora, I have another favor," Denise said. "I'm going to need a Spanish-speaking person in the campaign headquarters most of the time to help with the Latino vote. But I won't be able to pay them much money. A volunteer would be better."

"That'll be no problem. I can get plenty of volunteers for you. It's about time these politicians woke up to the fact that there is a Latino vote in this city."

"And can I count on you, Mira?"

"Sure can. You didn't even have to ask. In fact, Jeanette and I were talking about helping you last month when one of the staff asked us about the procedure for voter registration. Maybe we can have a candidates' night at the club. Let's talk about it after Nicky's wedding."

"Mira, you got a deal. Thanks so much."

◦ ◦ ◦

NICOLE ESCAPED to her bedroom. Freda was working her last nerve with her judgmental attitude toward Mira! Sometimes she could be so crass. She was going to talk to Freda about it after the wedding, but right now she needed to keep things light. But first, Nicole decided to give Tisha a call in spite of what Valerie had said earlier. The call went straight to Tisha's voice mail. *Maybe she turned the ringer off so that she and Kimmy can rest,* Nicole thought.

She decided to get back to her little soiree before Freda or Keisha demolished Valerie and Denise. Just as she reemerged into the living room, the phone rang. Valerie reached it first and announced that Renee was on her way up.

"Hey, Ms. Freda. What's up, girl?" Mira gave Freda a hug.

"Well, what do you know? It's SWV, Sisters *Without* Voices," Freda joked as she joined Keisha on the sofa and sipped on her drink while she looked at Zenora, Mira, and Valerie.

Keisha laughed and said, "Oh, that's some cold shit!"

Mira said, "That was cute, Freda. SWV, huh? I used to love their—"

Before Mira could finish, Freda interrupted, "I bet you did."

"—*music!*" Catching the eye of Zenora and Keisha, Mira smirked and asked, "So, Freda, tell us—when is your CD coming out? Oh, I'm sorry. You have to get a deal first."

Everyone knew Freda did not enjoy being the butt of jokes, especially when she wasn't the one telling them, so before Freda could respond, Mira warned, "Don't come for me, and I won't come for you." Mira walked toward Nicole and smiled as she handed over her gift. "Hey, baby, here you go."

"Aw, thanks, Mira! Oh, there's the door. It's Renee." Valerie opened the door for Renee, who burst in looking exhausted and talking on her cell phone. Renee gave a quick wave of the hand to everyone and headed to the bar.

Nicole said to Mira, "But you know you didn't have to buy me anything."

From across the room, Keisha shouted, "Yes, she did! What is it?"

Nicole, ignoring her, turned her attention back to Mira. "Where's Jeanette?"

"Home. She's taking it really bad."

Valerie hugged Mira and asked, "What, the flood?"

"No, she's dealing with that shit better than I am. She's more upset that we couldn't have Nicky's party at our club tonight. She had been decorating for it up to the last few days. Then the pipe burst in the basement, which sort of ruined everything, especially since she had discovered a small leak over a week ago. As a matter of fact, we made an appointment for a plumber to come out this coming Monday. So until then, the water has been shut off in the entire building."

"How's that going to affect the business in terms of you guys being open all next week?" Zenora asked.

"I really don't know. It's really now just a wait-and-see situation."

Sensing her chance to get back at Mira, Freda added, "Well, from a legal standpoint I hope you guys—oops, no pun intended!—I mean, you girls, have really good insurance, because if there is any other water damage outside of your building, it can be very costly. What do you think, Denise?"

"That's absolutely correct."

"No, we're cool. I believe we're gonna be okay in that area. Basically the damage appears to have been confined to our basement, but that didn't stop Jeanette from feeling she is to blame. I tried talking her into coming out tonight, but she said she wouldn't be much fun. Besides she knew this was Nicky's bachelorette party and felt I should just hang out alone with my girls tonight."

"The change of venue certainly wasn't her fault. We all understand. Besides, since it's just gonna be us, there was no reason why we couldn't have it here at my place."

"See there, Nicky, Mira understands. None of us were supposed to bring our *men*. I mean, our significant others. I have got to learn how to be more politically correct," Freda said.

In a warning tone, Nicole said, "One more time, Freda. One more time."

Mira interrupted, laughing. "Nicky, it's okay. I know Freda's got jokes. She's just trying to be funny." She gave Freda the finger.

"Now, did y'all see that?" Freda yelled. "I was trying to be nice, and Mira takes it to another level by giving me the middle finger."

"Oh, shit," Keisha said. "This is turning into a bad stage production of an all-black version of *Cats*." Noticing that Renee was still on her phone call as she passed her on the way to the bar, Keisha added, "Bitch, get off the phone.

You're rude. You're at somebody else's house. Ain't shit that important. *Get off the phone!*"

Putting her phone on mute, Renee lit into Keisha. "Keisha, I am taking a very important phone call about my career. It's my agent. Now I realize that you live *your* life through the celebrity of others, but *I am one.* So do me a favor. Get lost. Thanks, dear." And with that, Renee resumed her call. "Sorry, Josh. Sure. I'll be available on Monday. Ten o'clock, you say? Josh, be a doll and try to arrange for it to be pushed back to at least eleven. I won't get back in Manhattan until late Sunday night, and ten o'clock is just not going to work." Renee listened for a moment and apparently did not like the response, because she said, "Well, that's what I pay you for, Josh. Make it happen." Her call continued as she walked out of the room.

Mira said to Freda, "No, I just feel that with comedy in your act, you might get a little more attention. I mean, Rosie O'Donnell started out as a comedian, but she also does Broadway musicals, and she can't sing either. You shouldn't limit yourself, baby."

Sensing that Freda needed a lifeline, Keisha tried to assist. "Perfect example, Mira. Rosie O'Donnell, huh? You two have so much in common."

"Okay, stop it!" Nicole said, exasperated. "Everyone! Denise, you're not even helping me with this."

"Why should I help? I say let these cats claw till we see blood. And whoever wants me to represent them and shows me their purse, I'm on board."

Everyone laughed.

Renee reentered the room, happy as a lark. She sashayed her way over to Nicole, tossing her long blond tresses over her shoulder and sporting fake eyelashes as long as Venetian blinds. She handed her gift to Nicole. "I wish you and Alan all the best, Nicky."

"Oh, thanks, Ree Ree," Nicole said, giving her a hug.

Renee joined the other girls on the sofa. "I'm waiting for the day when I meet my Prince Charming."

Keisha snorted. "You mean your *white* knight in shining armor, don't you?"

"I meant Prince Charming, Keisha. No one said anything about color. That's your hang-up, not mine." Not missing a beat, Renee turned her attention to Nicole's hair. "Oh, your hair looks fabu! Those highlights do so much for you. You remind me of a darker-skinned Jennifer Aniston. Gosh, Zenora really hooked you up. Great job, Z."

Keisha, still fixated on Renee's comment, said, "Hold up, bitch. My hang-up?"

"Yes, your hang-up. I just choose to date white guys, that's all. *Brothas* just don't do it for me."

Mira giggled hysterically and said, "I know what you mean."

"It's not racial, just a preference. Besides—been there, done that. Renee DeVoe doesn't apologize to anyone because of whom she dates. I know what I like."

Zenora maneuvered her ample hips on the edge of the sofa, shifting, and offered her thoughts: "You know my take on all that. As long as he is slim, over six feet, has a job, owns a car, can spell *cat*—'cuz I'm too old to be a kitty—and has at least eight, I really don't care what nationality he is."

Looking toward Zenora, Valerie innocently asked, "eight what?" which sent the entire room into hysterical laughter.

An annoyed Zenora answered, "Teeth, Val! Eight teeth!"

Still confused, Valerie searched for an answer from one of the faces in the room.

Nicole said, "Pay Z no mind."

"Z, we all know you're Ms. United Nations. But I thought you were just into the *chulos*," Freda teased.

"True. But ain't no shame in my game. I'm serious—size does matter with my ass—but I do prefer Latinos."

Denise's cell phone went off. She considered letting it go directly to voice mail, but then remembered that it could be Domenick calling about the painters, so she answered it. "Hello? Yes, this is Denise. Hold on a second." She nodded at Nicole and went into her bedroom to take the call while the girls continued their conversation.

"What's so special about Latin men? I think Enrique Iglesias is really cute. I saw him perform live during the Puerto Rican Day Parade in Philly last summer, and he was so sweet. I still have the signed picture in my apartment. 'To Val, from Enrique.'"

"He's a little young for me, but I think he's okay. As far as what makes Latin men so special? We ain't got all night. Besides, this is supposed to be Nicky's night, not Zenora's sex secrets revealed."

Denise returned to the room with an annoyed expression on her face. "Well, it looks as though we're going to have to wait a little longer for my gift, Nicky. It seems my surprise was delivered to the Loose Balloon. The change in venue was obviously not communicated. Jeanette signed for it, and I'll pick it up later."

Nicole probed, "Denise, what are you doing? Have you hired strippers? Because if you have, I told you guys that I—"

"Calm down, it will be well worth it—you'll see. So what's this I hear about Zenora's sex secrets?"

Crunching on a carrot stick from the vegetable tray, Keisha said, "Oh, Ms. Z was just making mention of the fact of how Latin men were the shit."

"Really? I'd like to hear more about that."

"Yeah, girl. Personally, I've had more luck with them in the romance department. The sex is great, of course, but there's so much more to it than sex. We all know I'm a romantic." A round of heavy sighs, snickering, rolling of the eyes, and laughter filled the room as Zenora continued. "The attention they give me, not being afraid to show their sensitive side—that's a turn-on for me."

"*Sensitive* usually means he's in touch with his feminine side," Freda said. "What, he wants you to suck on his nipples and put your thumb up his ass? 'Cuz I heard those Spanish boys be into that freaky shit."

"Well, we all know you know about the freaky shit, don't we, Ms. Freda? So I'm sure whatever Z is doing, you can top it," said Keisha.

Valerie slipped out of the room, not wanting to hear

any of the sex talk, and she took a seat on the patio to get some air.

"No, I'm talking about *sensitive*. You know, like he might cry with me during a romantic movie, or allow me to hold him after making love instead of him always having to hold me. He'll wine and dine me, tell me his fears and dreams—"

"Oh, I feel you. In other words, you just want a bona fide sissy, huh?"

"No, she doesn't," Renee said, rolling her eyes. "I feel you on that, Zenora. It isn't always just about hitting it and then rolling over to sleep. White guys treat me with respect and tender loving care, like a delicate flower, and I like that. I'm special, and I deserve to feel that way all the time. I demand it on the set at work from my colleagues, my friends, family. It's a given. It's about respect, something I was never given when I dated black guys. I mean, there's only been two that I can really remember dating since I've been an adult. But even that was two too many."

"Now, wait a minute. There are plenty of brothas that do the same thing," Nicole said as Denise, Freda, and Keisha shook their heads affirmatively. "I mean, my Alan is very sensitive and caring in and outside of the bedroom. I like the fact that he is very tender with me. This may sound strange, but Alan makes love like a woman."

The room became silent.

Cautious looks were thrown around the room as each of the women tried to figure out what in the hell Nicole meant by that.

Denise decided that it was a good time for her to join

Valerie on the patio for some air. She took her phone with her to attempt to track down Domenick once more.

"It's not all physical, but emotional as well, girls." Nicole laughed.

"S-H-I-T, Ms. Keisha ain't gon' lie. Wining and dining and bringing me flowers is cute and thoughtful, but girls, sometimes I likes it raw. Shit yeah, y'all know what I'm talking about. Sometimes you just want a brotha to rip your panties off with his teeth, like a toddler opening gifts on Christmas morning."

The sound of laughter from inside carried to the patio where Denise and Valerie were talking.

"Hey, Val, you okay?"

Looking over the skyline of the city, Valerie answered softly, "Oh yeah, Denise, I'm okay. It's just been a really, really long day. I don't want my mood to spoil the evening for everyone else, but I just can't get my mind off the closing this morning at the Realtor's."

"Oh yes, how did that go?"

"It didn't. Without going too much into it, let's just say the seller didn't have all the legal paperwork. And with it being Friday, nothing can be done until Monday morning."

"Well, the good thing is at least your dream of owning your own day care center is becoming a reality. Monday may seem a ways off, but a lot can happen between now and then. It's something that you have worked toward for such a long time, so forty-eight hours is not going to make a difference in determining the fate of your future."

"I know, I know. But when you're so close to something and it means so much to your heart like this does—when there's a fork in the road, if you're not careful, the anxiety and stress will get the best of you."

"Oh, you don't have to tell me about stress and anxiety. Even with cutting down the number of cases that I have taken on in the last year, fund-raising and my campaign, at times, have been more than I can deal with."

"You'll do fine. You've always been able to handle the everyday trials and tribulations of life with ease. This will be no exception. I've admired your tenacity, your go-get-it spirit, since we were in school."

"Thanks, Val, but even I sometimes wonder if it's all really worth it."

"Of course it is. You are one of the most recognizable and prominent women in the city of Philadelphia. Whatever's happening, it will only be a minor setback, I'm sure."

For the first time in a long time, Denise felt her eyes well up. Still keeping her composure, she turned to Val. "That means more to me than you'll ever know, especially coming from you. Because I know that's a good place. So, changing the subject, missy—if there's anything I can do to make things run smoother on Monday from a legal angle, call me. No matter how busy I am, we'll get it done."

Denise's cell phone started to ring. She looked at the keypad. Domenick. "Finally," she said. "Hello, Domenick. What's going on? Did you get my message?" She listened carefully to his explanation. "Okay. As long as it's taken care of tomorrow, I'll be fine with it. No need to apologize. Mistakes happen. Okay. Thanks a lot. I will talk to you on Monday." She hung up the phone and let out a heavy sigh.

"Problem?"

"Problem solved. For now, that is."

Ten

Stranger in My House

THE WOMEN INSIDE were still in conversation about men, and Zenora had taken center stage. Swaying her hips and arms rhythmically from left to right, she began, "Yeah, treat me like the queen I am, and handle this fine brown frame. Massage my feet, baby—suck on my toes, *papi*—nibble on my—" Now well under the influence of alcohol, Keisha and Freda testified with shouts of approval and glee.

Freda jumped to her feet like she was at a Holy Ghost revival. "Okay, that's enough. You're getting my ass all hot up in here. Hallelujah and amen!"

The women fell out, fanning themselves like they had just been saved and born again—except for Mira, who used the opportunity to taunt Freda. "Oh, really now?"

Freda snapped back to reality. She composed herself

and threw a warning look at Mira as she shouted, "Oh, hell to the naw! You better sit yo' ass down somewhere. The only fish I like is from Bookbinders Seafood restaurant down on Delaware Ave."

Zenora—stretched out on the floor on her back, cooling herself off with a magazine, and repeating something totally inaudible in Spanish—managed to say to Renee, "Speaking of Latin men, what's up with that fine Spanish snack on your soap opera? Jorge Medina."

Renee, midway through making herself a margarita, responded, "First of all, he's black." Renee's pronunciation—*block*—never failed to raise an eyebrow. "He plays Latino. Mr. Medina's real name is Jackson Weldon, and I am not feeling him."

The combination of alcohol and her weight caused Zenora to struggle to get up off the floor. Holding on to both the coffee table and the edge of the sofa, she pulled herself up. Sitting back on the sofa, she said to Renee, "Well, girl, he is fine."

"I'll admit, he has his fans. I'm just not one of them. Of course, I had to get at him straight from jump. I was like, 'You, listen up. Unfortunately for me, we have to do this love scene, but I need you to remember, this is all acting. When that director yells *cut,* that's exactly what that means.' God! He pissed me off today because during the kissing scene, he went too far and tried to tongue me. Oh, my God, I'm actually getting sick again." Renee laid her head back on the sofa cushions.

Keisha said to Freda under her breath, "This bitch is too

fucking dramatic. Don't you just want to slap the hell out of her?" Laughing, Freda and Keisha laid their heads against each other and continued to watch Renee's performance.

"Yeah, but first, I just wanna go over there and snatch that blond weave out of her head and take those contacts out," Freda said. "On second thought, you know what would be better than that? When we leave tonight, let's just take her ass up to the worst part of Camden and just drop her ass off."

Keisha couldn't stop laughing but managed to get one last thing out. "Naw, girl, we can't. Nicky would be one girl short tomorrow at the wedding, and she would never forgive us. So let's just let the bitch live. It could be worse—she could still be living in Philly instead of New York, and we'd have to tolerate her ass all the time. So let's thank God for small blessings."

"Yeah, Keish, but you gotta love her."

"I do. But I still want to slap the shit out of her sometimes—like right now."

"Well," Nicole started, "I've seen Mr. Medina. He is rather good-looking, but—"

Sensing what Nicole was about to say, all the women chimed in. "We know: You only have eyes for Alan." Nicole playfully referred to them as haters.

"Why do all black men think it's just about getting laid?" Renee said as Denise and Valerie came in from the patio.

Denise answered, "Honey, all men think it's about getting laid."

Denise sat down next to Mira, who added, "You got that right, even the ones on the DL."

The mere mention of men on the DL appeared to sober up Zenora. "You do not want me to go there! Now that's some shit I do not understand."

"What's that, Z?" asked Nicole.

"This whole down-low phase."

"Ain't nothing new about men creeping with men. It's just getting more attention now because motherfuckers are getting caught," offered Keisha.

"Shit, y'all would be surprised at all the men that do that," said Mira. "A few of them come by my club, but I can spot one a mile away." Pointing with one hand to the left and one hand to the right she said, "There go D, and there go L." Bringing both hands to meet in the middle, she slapped them together and said, "DL."

"I know that's right. I didn't need that queen to write a book glorifying that shit—like he was helping us out. That Negro was trying to make a dollar," remarked Freda.

"J. L. King or something, right?" Denise asked. "A lot of the women at my law firm were reading it."

"So what did you think after *you* read it, Denise?" Valerie asked.

"You cannot possibly believe that I would waste my time reading that trash! Absolutely not. The subject does not interest me."

Between sips of her wine, Renee said, "Well, it should, Denny—especially if you're dating."

"Excuse me, but I know the men I screw, Ms. DeVoe."

Rising up off the love seat on her way to grab a beer, Mira said, "Yeah, but do you know the men that screw you?"

"Terry McMillan thought she knew that shit, too," Keisha said. "Did y'all see *Oprah*? Chile, I knew when I first saw him that he was a switch-hitter. Eyebrows were done up better than mine, and that soft-as-Michael-Jackson voice. I was like, 'Girl, please, don't you see what this is?' And did you see how mad Terry looked when she had to sit next to him in front of all those millions of people? I would've been mad, too, if a nigga had on more lip gloss than I did."

"But you know what?" Freda said. "I really do believe that she loved him. And I'm not gonna say that he didn't love her, although I really do believe, at the end of the day, it was just about getting that green card."

"Well, he would have got a green card and an ass-whooping, 'cuz Ms. Keisha don't play that shit. I don't have anything against gay men. Some of my best girlfriends are gay men, and I'm not gon' say that I know for sure that every man I've been with is straight-up heterosexual, but if I find out that him and I are liking the same thing, I'm puttin' my foot up his ass and then I'm gone."

"Which leads me to say something here, ladies," Keisha said. "I never understood how a woman can let a man that she meets run up in her without a trench coat on in 2008. Because I'ma tell you how I handle that shit. When I meet me somebody, I don't care how fine he looks, before he puts his wallet in my pocketbook, I'ma see what that shit's made of. In other words, the light is gonna be on, and I'm gon' have to handle that—examining, lifting, twisting, turning, and flipping. I did not live to be thirty years old by being a fool."

Denise stood up and made her way over to the bar. "Okay, I've heard enough. I need another drink. We are supposed to be here to party, not have an *Oprah* start-up support group."

"Exactly. Nicky, by any chance do you have Eric Benet's last CD?" Zenora made her way over to the walnut-finished CD case, which housed over three hundred CDs, ranging from Bach to T.I. Even though the CDs were alphabetically organized, Zenora was too tipsy to find the CD she was looking for.

Nicole went over to assist her friend and found the album right away.

The mere mention of Eric Benet's name, however, sent Freda into a tizzy. "Hell naw! His shit is too mellow and depressing. I don't feel like that right now. Put on some Nelly or Usher. Besides, I don't wanna hear some nigga crying about how he fucked up on fourteen songs!"

Nicole rolled her eyes and took back the CD from Zenora and found another. Soon a slow, sexy ballad by Usher filled the room, and each woman started to sway and groove to the music. A few of them sang along.

Denise, sitting in one of the chairs at the dining room table, took a quick glance around the room, and it hit her that Tisha was not there. "Hey, where's Tisha?"

"Oh, that's right, you girls weren't here," Nicole answered. "She called earlier. Valerie got the call, and Tisha told her that because of her migraines, she probably wouldn't make it tonight."

"Tisha's not coming? That's a bummer," Renee said.

Zenora stood up and started to pace. She appeared to be struggling with something and asked, "Can I say something?"

Everyone's attention went to Zenora. Freda was the first to speak. "Yeah, what's up?"

"Ah, never mind. I'm probably just tripping. It's nothing," Zenora said, feeling put on the spot. *Maybe it's best to leave it alone,* she thought.

"Say what's on your mind, Z," Nicole said. "We're all family here."

Usher continued to sing in the background as everyone sat and waited for Zenora to speak. She went over to the sound system, turned off the music, and with her back to the other girls, she pondered how to begin.

Speaking hesitantly, she said, "The other day Tisha came by the shop to get her hair done, and I noticed some marks around her neck." Zenora started pacing and eventually made her way to the bar for another drink. No one else said anything as they hung on to her every word. "I have to be honest—I tried to ignore it, but I couldn't. When I asked her about it, she started crying."

Mira said through clenched teeth, "If that bastard hit Tisha, I will personally cut his ass!"

Zenora continued, "I pleaded with her. I said, 'Tisha, did Roland do this to you?' She snapped at me saying, 'No, he didn't, and I would appreciate it if you would just leave it alone. And don't say anything to the other girls, because it's not what you think.' "

Feeling even more guilty than before, Zenora said, "She made me swear that I would keep my suspicions to myself. I told her if she needed a place for herself and Kimmy to go, they could stay with me. That seemed to make her angrier. She jumped up, wrote me a check, and stormed out. Her hair wasn't even done yet. She just ignored me. I was hoping to see her tonight to tell her I was sorry and that maybe I did jump the gun. Maybe my accusations were incorrect."

Denise immediately got up and went to get her purse. "I would say your accusations were right on target, Zenora. We all know that he has hit her before, so let's not pretend to deny that. Listen, you guys start eating. I'll be back."

Realizing what she may have started, Zenora attempted to prevent Denise from leaving. "I know where you're going. Please don't do it. I gave her my word."

Mira became furious with Zenora. "Bitch, are you crazy? This is serious. The reason why Tisha isn't here tonight is because he probably hit her again. Come on, Denise, let's go!" Mira searched through her purse, frantically trying to locate something, which irritated Denise.

"You won't need your keys, Mira. I'll drive," Denise said impatiently.

"Keys? I know where the hell my keys are. I'm making sure I got my shit with me." She flashed a switchblade and headed toward the door.

"Maybe before you two go over there, I should call and check on Tisha first," Nicole said, not wanting any trouble for anyone. Renee, Keisha, Valerie, and Freda agreed it would be the best thing to do. However, nothing seemed to convince Denise or Mira, who'd already decided they were leaving.

"Call, my ass. Come on, Denise," Mira said.

As they reached the door, Nicole's buzzer rang. She quickly went to see who it was. "It's Tisha," she said, surprised and relieved as she buzzed her friend in.

While everyone waited for Tisha to take the elevator up to her nineteenth-floor condo, Nicole pleaded, "Okay, guys, do not jump to any conclusions." Mira rolled her eyes, and Denise folded her arms. "Just allow Tisha to offer any information, good or bad, herself."

Everyone agreed, and Mira reluctantly returned her knife to her purse. The women tried to sit around the room and act as if everything were normal and waited for Tisha to come in.

○ ○ ○

TISHA TOOK OUT her compact on the elevator to double-check her appearance in the mirror. It was obvious by the redness of her eyes that she'd been crying. She adjusted the orange-and-gold scarf around her neck, tucking the ends of it into her crisp white button-down blouse and made sure that her neck was not visible. Chic designer jeans graced her slim frame and her three-and-a-quarter-inch gold strappy Jimmy Choo stilettos accented with a gold clutch bag complemented her outfit. She looked better than she felt. Going to the party was a last-minute decision, so she'd forgotten to bring Nicole's gift. As the elevator doors opened, she took a deep breath and put her game face on, rehearsing her story. When she turned the corner, Nicole was already in the hallway waiting for her, ready to greet Tisha alone. The sight of Nicole in the hall caught Tisha off guard.

"Hey, Tish."

"What's up, Nicky? What are you doing in the hall?"

"Oh, nothing. Just wanted to make sure you were okay."

"Why wouldn't I be okay?"

Nicole stared at Tish for a moment, wanting to probe further. Opting instead to hug her, Nicole said, "I'm so glad you're here. The girls are going to be so happy to see you." When they entered the apartment, all eyes immediately turned to Tisha who became uneasy at the way her friends were looking at her.

"Isn't there a party going on here tonight? No music, no laughter?" Tisha asked.

A heavy silence settled over the room.

Renee spoke first and went over to give Tisha a hug. "Hey, Tish. You feeling better?"

"Oh yeah, girl, just one of my migraines. But I took my medicine and laid down for a while. I'm sure Valerie told you guys that I wasn't coming. But after waking up, I felt better, and the thought of not being here with my girls on such an important night for our girl Nicole wasn't even an option."

Mira seemed unconvinced as she asked from across the room, "Where are Roland and Kimmy?"

"Roland worked late tonight. I left him a note reminding him of Nicky's party," Tisha said nonchalantly. "And I dropped Kimmy off at my grandma's."

More silence.

Judging by the looks on everyone's faces, Tisha could tell that no one believed her. "Why are all of you looking at me like that?"

After searching the room, she fixed on Zenora, and their eyes met. Tisha asked, "Zenora, did you—?"

However, before she finished her question, Denise jumped in. "Did she what?"

Tisha tried to play it off. "Did Zenora tell you I got mad at her the other day at the shop and flipped out?" Before anyone had a chance to answer, she continued, "Girl, I'm sorry. It was all a misunderstanding." Tisha hugged Zenora and then threw a dirty look visible only to Zenora. Turning back to the other girls, she asked, "Hey, can we get some music up in here to liven up this place? Y'all standing around looking like you on *The Golden Girls*. Let me go over here and see what kind of music you got in this case, Ms. Nicky. I need to find something to get us in the party mood."

She selected an up-tempo old-school song that was a favorite of the crew when they would go out to party. Once the song began, Tisha started dancing and coaxing the other girls to join in the fun. Their dance moves consisted of all the dances they did in high school and college. Keisha did the cabbage patch; Freda, the running man; Denise, the snake; and Renee, the prep. They made a *Soul Train* line.

After having the same song on repeat several times, they began to wind down, and Tisha made her way over to the bar to get a drink. It was clear that she was still pissed at Zenora. Noticing that Tisha had quietly slipped away from the party activity, Zenora decided to join her at the bar to offer her apologies.

On the other side of the room, Nicole started to describe her wedding dress and showed them a picture of the dress in a *Modern Bride* magazine. Their reactions indicated that they approved of her choice. She then invited the women into her bedroom to show them the actual dress. They all headed in, and Valerie called out to Zenora and Tisha. "Hey, guys, come see Nicky's dress." The two glanced over, nodded, and gestured that they would—but first they had to clear the air.

"I know you told them what you thought you saw!"

"Tisha, I—" Zenora started to say.

"Shut up! The only reason that I did not go off a few minutes ago is because I would not do anything to spoil Nicky's night. You just couldn't leave it alone, could you, Z? Is it so hard for you to mind your own business?" Tisha made herself a cocktail. She noticed that there was no ice, but decided to drink it anyway. "What goes on in my house is my business. Roland did not hit me."

"Tisha, I'm sorry—"

"You should be!"

"But when I saw those marks on your neck, I assumed—"

Before Zenora could complete her sentence, Tisha threw the remainder of her drink at her. "Well, you assumed wrong! If you must know, the marks on my neck were from a little rough lovemaking between me and my man. I'm sure you can understand what a little rough fucking can result in, especially with all the various sexual partners that you've had. I'm sure at least one of them got a little rough."

Grabbing a towel off the bar, Zenora calmly wiped herself off and addressed Tisha. "I'm going to attribute what you just did to all that you are obviously going through and not knock you the hell out. I understand that I was wrong in mentioning anything to the girls, but it was clearly out of love and concern that I did say anything."

"Well, I don't need that kind of love, Zenora. So I'd appreciate you staying out of my personal affairs."

"You will never have to worry about that again. I apologize that I didn't warn you that I was going to say something to the other girls, but I'm *not* sorry that I did it."

With her back to Zenora, Tisha's eyes welled up, and although she wanted to reach out and say more, fear got the best of her.

Mira came back into the living room to retrieve her camera and sensed something was wrong between Tisha and Zenora. After approaching them, she noticed that the top of Zenora's blouse was all wet.

"Aren't you guys gonna come back and see Nicky's dress?" Mira asked. Neither one of them responded.

"How did you get all wet?" Mira asked Zenora.

"That was my fault," Tisha said. "Z startled me when she came over to get a drink, and I just threw it on her. It was a mistake. Right, Z?"

Zenora just glared at Tisha for a moment, turned toward Mira, and excused herself. She'd decided to go to the patio to cool down.

"What's going on, Tisha?" Mira demanded.

"Nothing. Nothing is going on." Tisha turned toward Mira. "Why does anything have to be going on?"

Grabbing Tisha by both arms, Mira continued, "Be quiet and listen to me. I know what's been going on at your house. We all know that Roland has been hitting on you. Now if you want to throw a drink on me or get mad at me, then go ahead, but I am not going to stand around and allow that motherfucker to hit you and get away with it. Any man that hits on a woman is a punk. I know that Kimmy is only six months old and may not have a clue about what's going on, but what are you going to say when he starts hitting on her, huh?"

"You don't know what you're talking about! Now I don't know what Z told you guys, but I'm going to tell you what I told her. Mind your own damn business. You need to concern yourself with yours and Jeanette's affairs, and not mine."

Raising her voice, Mira pointed at Tisha. "No, I need you to wake the fuck up, Tish!" Their voices began to escalate loud enough to draw the others into the living room. The women raced back to see what was happening.

Nicole was the first to speak. "Hey, hey, what's going on in here? Mira? Tish? What's the matter?"

Mira said, "Nothing. Everything is cool. So, Nicky, let's open those gifts." She glanced back disgustedly at Tisha before walking over to the group.

Eleven

Girls Just Wanna Have Fun

RENEE GATHERED the presents from the dining room table and brought them to the sofa for Nicole to open.

Denise interjected, "No, no, no, it's not fair to open the gifts until all gifts are present. No pun intended. Now we'll wait a little longer, eat some more, play some games."

"Anyone for charades or Trivial Pursuit? Or how about Life?" Nicole said.

Freda said, "Aww, hell to the naw. Oh hell, charades? Life? I play life every day I wake up. All we're doing is sittin' around drinking."

Keisha said, "How about Hollywood Dream Hookup?"

Renee answered, "Hollywood what?"

Keisha explained, "Hollywood Dream Hookup. It's

simple. We will each throw out the name of a Hollywood male star—someone who we think is hot."

Mira said, "Aw, shit—I'm out unless y'all gonna name some sistahs, too."

"Hell no. We're naming men," Freda said.

Mira replied jokingly, "I'll play along. Just because I'm a lesbian doesn't mean I don't appreciate beauty—even if it's in a man."

"You'll need a moderator, so naturally I'm good at stuff like that," Denise said. "What are the rules, Keisha?"

"We name an actor or singer who is hot," explained Keisha, "and then we rate them one to ten. I'll go first. Denzel Washington."

Denise said, "Fine, just fine. A ten!"

They all agreed except for Freda, who frowned and commented, "Yeah, but he looks like he can only go one round a night, then he's done."

"Okay, do you mean *Training Day* Denzel or *Preacher's Wife* Denzel? Because if you mean *Training Day* Denzel, panties down," Keisha stated.

"My turn," Zenora said, rolling her eyes at Keisha's antics. "Blair Underwood, also fine. A nine, but I always felt you can't touch his hair. It's always perfect."

"You mean it's always greasy," interjected Keisha. "He needs to let that perm go."

"I've got one," Renee spoke excitedly in her high-pitched tone. "Justin Timberlake!"

Most of the women frowned, but Tisha backed her up. "I'll give you that one. I think he's an eight and a half."

"Man, he couldn't handle a sistah," Zenora said, shaking her head. "He reminds me of a little boy. And another thing, he can *take* sexy back."

"Okay, me, me, here's my choice," said Nicole. "Will Smith! Nice, sexy, cute—I'd give Will a nine and a half."

Valerie said, "He's a ten for me. All women love Will Smith. He's handsome, funny, rich, and he's a good father. He provides, and he's an overachiever."

Freda jumped in and asked Valerie, "Bitch, are you his publicist?"

Tisha thought Smith was gentle in a manly way. Her fantasy about him was definitely far from the real-life brutality she got at home from Roland. She daydreamed and thought how wonderful it would be to have a husband who was gentle. He doesn't have to be rich or famous, just gentle. She thought, *Roland's brutal hands and harsh words are probably his only way to show that he loves me, maybe?*

Denise expressed admiration for his wife, Jada Pinkett Smith. "She's a woman in her own right. If I married him, I wouldn't give up my law practice and political career, just like Jada didn't give up her career."

Keisha told Denise, "You got two chances to marry Will Smith: slim and none. Besides, a brotha got to come correct with Miss Jada. She don't care how much he got. If he's not delivering in the bedroom, sistah girl would have stepped. I believe that shit."

"Hey, everybody, I got another one. Wesley Snipes," said Valerie.

The entire room became quiet as a mouse. The girls looked at each other and then turned to Valerie.

Keisha couldn't hold her tongue. "Are you crazy? He doesn't want you anyway. Hell to the naw—and his ass owes the government."

"Okay, okay, if I were to *ever* do a man, it would be Brad Pitt," confessed Mira.

"Ooooh, he's the hottest ever. Oh my God, oh my God," Renee shrieked, flustered and overjoyed at the thought.

Nicole said, "I'm feelin' you on that and did you see him in the movies *Troy* and *Fight Club*? Whew! Now that's one man worth crossing the color line for."

Denise said, "Me, too. Then there's Colin Farrell. We all know he likes sistahs and video cameras."

"Hold up. I got one for everybody: Mr. LL Cool J," said Freda. "I may not be his round-the-way girl, but I'll be his up-the-block bitch."

"Hell to the yeah!" everyone said, before chiming in to sing one of his songs:

"Standing at the bus stop, suckin' on a lollipop."

Then Valerie added, *"Once she gets pumpin', it's hard to make the hottie stop—"*

Surprised, the other women yelled, "Whoa—Go, Val! Go, Val! Go, Val!"

"I can't believe I did that," Val said, amazed.

"Yeah, chile, if I wasn't getting married tomorrow, LL Cool J could get it. Ouch!" Nicole threw her long legs in the air like two stiff boards.

Denise looked over at Tisha and said, "Tish, you with us?"

"Oh yeah, yeah, I was just fantasizing about . . . oh, never mind. Okay, who has the best body and face in Hollywood but people usually hate him? Can't guess? Okay, Shemar Moore."

"Oh no," Freda said. "He's overrated, and I ain't really feelin' those light-skinned brothas. The same for that Boris Kodjoe."

"Are you crazy? They are too fine!" Tish offered.

"But for body, give me Tyrese any day," Zenora said.

Keisha broke in again. "Chile, please. He look like a lizard in the face." She imitated the movement of a scaly lizard creature by thrusting out and wagging her tongue from side to side.

"You're so ignorant, Keisha," Freda said, and shook her head.

Valerie said, "But I thought Tyrese was sexy-bad in that movie, *Baby Boy*. You know, like he's sexy, but so bad."

"Stop, Val, you sound ridiculous," Denise said.

Renee came up with another choice, "How about Ricky Martin?"

"Sweet as cake," Keisha said.

Freda concurred, "Like Duncan Hines."

"He is not, Keisha," admonished Renee. "There you go again with those ridiculous rumors."

"Hell to the naw" was the response for Tom Cruise, but for Morris Chestnut it was another story.

Freda said, "He's rich, beautiful chocolate," and then

made a hissing noise like a whistling teakettle. "I wanna have his kids."

"I hate to throw a wrench in your fantasy, but he's married," Valerie said.

"And?" Freda responded. "I said, I wanna have his kids."

"Okay, time for one more, and all kidding aside," Keisha announced. "You are going to think I'm crazy, but you know who I think will give you the time of your life?"

Everyone asked, "Who?"

"Jimmy J. J. Walker!"

Hysterical laughter followed. Renee asked, "What? Do you mean that string bean from *Good Times*?"

"Have you lost your mind?" Freda asked. "You *must* be crazy. How many drinks have you had? Why him?"

"You all naming those pretty boys that will be fighting yo' ass for mirror time. But if you get somebody as ugly as J.J. and give his ass some, he'll tear your shit up! Raw, chile. And with those soup cooler lips? Chile, please."

There was a knock at the door.

Freda jumped to the door. "Who is it?"

"Security!" a deep voice called out from the other side of the door.

Nicole wondered why building security would come to her apartment. Freda opened the door, and in entered a six-foot-tall, mocha-chocolate muscular-framed man wearing heavy-duty black boots and a tight black T-shirt with the words SECURITY in bold white letters on his broad chest. His chiseled facial features enhanced a pencil-thin mustache and deep-set dark eyes. He held a flashlight in one hand, which gave him an air of authority, but the duffel bag in the other brought a question to Nicole's mind. She had never seen this security man in her four years of living in the condo. There was a brand of a horseshoe on his upper arms, which indicated that he was a Q DOG.

He said, "Excuse me, ladies. We've gotten some complaints that there is some sort of party going on here. Loud music, laughter—you know, the usual."

Perplexed, Nicole said, "But we don't have any music on."

He retorted, "You're having a party and no music?"

Nicole answered, "There was music on before, but we're just laughing and having fun. That's all."

"Do you mind if I check the volume button on your sound system?"

"Oh my God, this is really insane," Nicole said. "This makes no sense at all."

"Now, now, Nicky," said Zenora, "let the security officer do his job."

Nicole caught on and was eased over to the high-back chair while the others arranged themselves to get ready for the show. Freda pulled out dollar bills from her clutch, but Denise vacated to the patio. Mira decided to get another beer at the bar.

The guard pushed in his CD, and the music began. Keisha dimmed the lights.

"Ladies, are you ready for the Knight Rider? Who wants to take the first ride?"

In unison, the women hollered, "Yeah!" Freda signaled him to go to Mira, who was nursing her drink at the bar.

His body attempted to grind against Mira, who immediately sent him away to the action on the other side of the room with the girls. "I know you better get away from me. I don't even play that shit!" He was smart enough to move on.

Zenora captured his attention by standing in the middle of the floor. "Come here, *papi,*" she teased, signaling him with her finger. He swung her around, lifting her ample body with ease as she pulled off his black T-shirt to reveal his muscular tattooed frame encased in a tight white tank top. "Ah, shit—now don't break nothing, pa!" Zenora yelled out.

He then danced his way over to the sofa where Keisha, Tisha, and Renee were seated. They kept their eyes on his every grind and bopped to the rhythm of the music. He stalked his next partner. It was Tisha who took off her belt, wrapped it around his neck, and pulled him in like a cowgirl lassoing a steer.

Renee motioned for him to grab Keisha, who was still sitting on the sofa, but he had his own agenda. He grabbed Renee by the arm and bent her body forward. From behind, he held her hips and simulated sexual gyrations. It was too much for Renee, who told him to stop, so he slapped her on the butt and looked for his next victim. He leapt behind the sofa for Freda, who was waiting for him to have some fun with her. She enticed him with a seductive dance, pulled off his white tank top, and tossed it in the air. Tisha grabbed it like a prize.

Freda had done this stripper scene before, and she knew how to increase the fun. He spotted folded dollar bills sticking out from her bosom like leaves on a tree, but in this case, the leaves were five- and ten-dollar bills. She instructed him to take the money out *with his teeth,* and Knight Rider put on a show by sliding up and down her body like a snake. Each time he curled around her cleavage, a bill was removed. Once he secured all the bills with his teeth, she stuffed them into his black silk shorts, which tore away to reveal a bright pair of bikini briefs. "Oohh, what you got in them shorts? Huh? Let me see! Let me see!" Freda said.

The loud screams told the neighbors that someone was having lots of fun in that apartment.

Keisha awaited her turn by positioning herself on her back and stretching out on the sofa. Knight Rider read her body language and mounted her missionary-style, burying his face in her blouse. "Don't play with me, boy, 'cuz it's been a minute! I'll ride you like an amusement park roller coaster!" she screamed with delight.

Shoeless and shirtless, the stripper yanked Tisha from the sofa and lifted her high in the air with his face buried between her thighs. Then he changed her position, and she rode him like a bronco on his back while twirling that white tank top around like a flag. She dismounted her stallion, and he took center stage on the floor, where he worked the girls in a frenzy of gyrations and music. The hotter they got, the bigger their tips.

Freda grabbed a camera and started clicking away.

He then approached Val, who shook her head. "No, no, I can't. Go over there to one of them," Val pleaded. The other girls knew she was shy and embarrassed, but they taunted her to try. He moved over to her chair and straddled her facing him. He removed her hands from her face and placed them on his butt as he grinded to the music. Val kept her eyes closed and started to shake until her shoes came off! She wanted to enjoy the dance, but she didn't know how to let herself go.

Freda shouted, "Go with the flow!" and the rest of the women joined in with snapping fingers, "Go with the flow."

Knight Rider saved Nicole, the guest of honor, for last. He got on all fours and pranced over to her like a thoroughbred and motioned for her to hop on for a bronco ride. Wrapped up in the moment, Nicole temporarily forgot Alan. "I can't believe I'm doing this," she said as she took her ride.

Exhausted and satisfied, the six women recuperated while Knight Rider retreated to the bedroom for a change.

He danced to another popular song, a more sensual cool down. Freda continued to unload those bills from her purse as the others followed suit. Keisha, Freda, and Zenora were the most tipsy by that time. Valerie and Nicole were warm and fuzzy from the white wine, just enough to be relaxed, but more in control of themselves than the rest. Mira was very quiet, with something weighing on her mind; however, also working on her third beer.

After Knight Rider completed his act, he retreated to

Nicole's bedroom to get dressed in his street clothes. Denise came back in from the patio, and Renee approached her, saying giddily, "Denny, you missed all the fun!"

Denise looked at her. "Not really. And Renee, I really wish you would stop calling me Denny. My name is Denise."

"Whatever, Denise, party pooper."

"And another thing, I thought I was in charge of this party tonight. This whole Knight Rider thing was a complete farce. Nicole distinctly expressed no strippers at her bachelorette party, and I did not authorize it." Denise was frustrated. It had been a long day, and at that moment, she would rather have been at home soaking in a hot tub. This was one of the most disappointing days in a long, long time.

Renee was hurt and surprised at Denise's tone; however, the apple martinis made her care less about what Denise said to her. Renee was determined to have herself a good time this evening. She turned to Denise and again said, "Party pooper."

Zenora left the other women, who were recovering from Knight Rider, and made her way to Nicole's bedroom. She handed his CD to him and took five moist one-hundred-dollar bills from inside her lace bra.

"Well, ya know, we can do a little somethin' somethin' extra right here," he said as he gazed down at her oversized breasts and reached for the money.

"I think I'll pass. For one, out of respect for my girl's spot here, it just wouldn't feel right; and two, I got my own little thing going on later on when my *papi* comes through to touch me up, *comprende*."

"Hey, Knight Rider, you better hurry up out here and get back on this track, ha, ha," Freda hollered from the hallway.

"Did you hear that? See, my fans are callin' for more, and they want an encore," he said in a seductive whisper, so close, she could smell the cheap liquor on his breath.

"You're done here for tonight, playa," Zenora replied as she slowly stuffed his front pocket with the bills and managed to slip her hand toward his monstrous manhood. He smiled, but then took a moment to count the dollars left in his pocket. "Damn, cheap bitches," he said under his breath before he left the bedroom.

He stepped into the hallway as Denise approached the bedroom entrance. "Oh, you weren't feelin' Knight Rider, huh, baby?" He stroked her arm.

Denise glared. "Get your hands off of me!"

He complied and quickly stepped back while raising both hands and surrendering to her request; then he headed to the living room.

The girls were still reveling in Knight Rider's encounter and teasing one another about the escapade.

"Remember, ladies, I got the pictures to prove it, and pictures don't lie. So don't be saying you didn't enjoy this shit," Freda said.

"Oh God, don't tell Alan. No."

Keisha suggested, "Let's all wear that photo on T-shirts when we walk down the aisle instead of our bridesmaid gowns. Yeah, it can say I RODE KNIGHT RIDER, and Nicky's picture would be right on it in one hundred percent white cotton, nonshrinkable!"

"Oh, that's not right. Don't you dare do that. Whatever happens at Nicky's condo, *stays* at Nicky's condo," Nicole warned.

Mira laughed off their joke. "You bitches are crazy."

Zenora came from the bedroom and spied Denise putting cold water to her face. "Are you okay, Denise?"

Denise kicked the door, slamming it in Zenora's face.

She sat on the toilet seat, taking a few moments to compose herself and come up with an excuse to explain her behavior. She just wanted to get home and into that hot tub. But at that moment, the water running in the sink soothed her, even though it was a poor substitute.

Knight Rider bade them good-bye. "Okay, ladies, I'm out." His new fans said good-bye, and Freda and Keisha tucked away his business card for future use. As he left, he passed a tall muscular man in a uniform with a starched white shirt and work pants emerging from the elevator. Knight Rider said, " 'Sup, nigga. You here to dance, too? 'Cuz if you are, dem hoes is cheap, man. I see you got your hookup on, playa." He glanced up and down at the newcomer's attire.

Instead of answering him, the other man cold-cocked Knight Rider right in the mouth, drawing a mass of blood, which flowed down his yellow sweatshirt. The assailant kept walking toward apartment 1901 without even looking back.

Struggling to get up on his feet, Knight Rider cried, "What the *fuck* is wrong with you, man?"

The door to the apartment was open, and he walked in to dim lights, heavy laughter, and drinks flowing. The man surveyed the whole scene but did not take his eyes from Tisha—not for one moment.

"Tisha." No response. "Yo, Tish." He said this even louder and with more anger, getting the attention of everyone in the room, causing Denise to come out of the bathroom and ask Nicole, "How many people have keys to your place?"

"You might want to try locking your door." It was Roland.

Fear overcame Tisha, who scurried around to grab her shoes and handbag. She eyed her silk scarf on the floor and quickly tied it around her neck. Approaching her husband, she stuttered, "Hey, honey, you know everyone. Is everything okay? I left a note for you."

"Everything is fine. Let's go," he said.

Denise stopped in her tracks. "Wait a minute, Roland. We're still partying—everything isn't done."

"Tisha is done," Roland said, glaring at Denise. "Say good-bye to your friends, baby. You're a mother—you need to be home."

"Honey, I left Kimmy with Granny. She's fine. Uhmm, I was coming home in a little bit. May I stay with my girls?"

Freda blurted out, *"May I?"*

"Yeah, bitch," Roland said, turning around to stare at Freda, "she said, 'may I.'"

Freda removed her heels and earrings. "Oh no, he didn't. Muthafucka, I'll slap you to sleep."

Keisha picked up an empty wine bottle from the bar and stood ready for the confrontation.

Zenora and Nicole ran over to stop Freda, while a nervous Valerie remained by the bar for cover. Renee and Denise stood off to the side, each wondering guiltily if the inevitable ugly scene unfolding before them would affect their careers in a negative way.

Roland tried to take a different tack. "It's getting late and I don't want to worry about you leaving here all by yourself."

"I'll be all right. Somebody will walk me to my car."

Impatient, Roland grabbed Tisha's arm. "Get your shit, and wait in the lobby for me."

Mira angrily broke through the pack and approached Roland head on. "Get your hands off of her."

Tisha tried to aid the situation. "It's okay, Mira. Roland is right, I probably need to get going now. Kimmy will wake up and start crying."

"Are you going to be all right, Tish?" Denise asked, her face revealing her concern. She could tell Tisha was scared and embarrassed.

"I'll talk to—," Tisha said before Roland cut her off and pulled her to the door.

"Of course she's all right. She's with her family. Her *real* family," he said, looking over at Mira.

"Somebody's got to say something to this bastard. Roland, I know and you know that you are a poor excuse for a man and that any man who hits on a woman is a punk-ass bitch. We all know what's going on. We know you hit Tisha!" Mira shouted.

Roland stood over Mira and looked down on her. "Look at Mira tryin' to be the man up in this piece. Sorry, bitch, your dick ain't big enough."

Nicole retreated to the sofa—her nerves were getting the best of her.

Mira pushed Roland, and her shiny blue steel switch-blade jolted out from its case.

Nicole screamed, "I need you to leave, Roland. Just get out of my house now!"

"I'm leaving, and let me tell you menless bitches something: Tisha is my muthafuckin' wife. She does what the fuck I tell her to do. By the way, this is the last time you'll see her over here. You feel me?"

Mira wasn't going to let that go. "Tisha is a grown-ass woman, and she can come and go as she pleases."

"You know what, bitch, if you were a real man, I'd kick your muthafuckin' dyke ass."

Mira said, " 'N' if you were a real man, b-i-t-c-h, I'd be scared."

The women headed toward Roland—Keisha armed with her wine bottle, Freda with her stilettos, and Renee with a candy dish. Denise stepped in front and said, "And if Tisha ever decides to drop your ass, understand I will represent her and hang your ass out to dry. I will use all my power to have them send you to Graterford, where the brothas will take real good care of you."

Roland applauded Denise sarcastically before reaching in his pocket to pull out two one-dollar bills, which he then tried to shove in her cleavage, but Denise slapped his arm away. Roland let the money fall to the floor and applauded her response. "Good job, Denise. Good job." Then Roland made one last obscene gesture at Mira before leaving.

All the drama proved to be too much for Nicole. Her body started shaking, in the early stages of a diabetic attack.

"Quick, get something sweet—juice, candy, anything sweet. Now!" ordered Denise.

Valerie scurried to the refrigerator for juice, and Freda headed to the bathroom for a cold compress.

Twelve

Hurricane

ROLAND BERATED Tisha as soon as he shoved her in the car. He sped through the streets, running through traffic lights and narrowly missing a pedestrian crossing the avenue. Tisha was afraid to warn Roland about his reckless driving and was glad their baby was not in the car during his tirade.

Roland began to dig in. "You take the bus back to that ho's place to pick up yo' car tomorrow. I work all day, and you out here dancin'—out with hoes and dykes and strippers. That dyke is the only one who stood up for you. Are you fuckin' her, too? And *you,* the mother of my child? Bitch, you must be crazy if you think I'm going to put up with that shit. I married a ho."

Tisha knew she ought to remain stiff and quiet when

Roland reached this level of anger, but she tried feebly to defend herself. "Honey, I was just—"

"What? What did you say? I dare you to cry. What are you cryin' 'bout? What?"

"It was just a—"

"I didn't tell you to say shit. If I wasn't so tired, I'd throw your ass out this car." Roland spit in her face and then gave her a look that dared her to wipe it off. "You can't be no mother. You don't even look as good as you used to look. Better yet, I'm goin' to teach you a lesson when you get home. As soon as you get out this here car, take all of yo' clothes off because I'm goin' to give you a beatin' you'll never forget. Somebody's got to teach you a lesson. 'N' why you coverin' up yo' neck now? It wasn't covered up when I caught you shaking yo' ass in that apartment. If you think you got some marks on your neck now, wait till we get home, 'cuz I'm goin' to put some marks on yo' ass. You're too stupid to see that you're hangin' out with bitches who ain't got no man—and one of 'em thinks she is one. Then there's Nicky, who's goin' to marry some punk-ass doctor. But you're the only one who's got a man at home. Me."

Tisha was immune to his ranting. She had no more tears to give. Once inside the house, no words are spoken. Tisha headed straight upstairs with her head bowed low. She heard the click of Roland's large metal buckle releasing the belt from his pants. She knew what was coming and counted each step up the staircase.

Thirteen steps. Thirteen steps.

Downstairs, Roland poured a stiff drink of Cutty Sark Scotch. Courage. He knew he had to keep order in his house and in his life, just as his mother, Melba, had done. He ascended the stairs. Thirteen steps. His wide black belt wrapped around his hand. Roland walked into their bedroom, where Tisha was sitting, ready for her punishment.

He closed the door.

Thirteen

Someone to Watch Over Me

BACK AT NICOLE'S, everyone was in a very somber mood. Stress and anxiety had caused Nicole to have a diabetic attack. However, once the girls gave her something to drink and calmed her down, Nicole rested comfortably in her bedroom. A Musiq Soulchild cut from his latest CD played on the radio. Mira was outside smoking a cigarette, resuming a bad habit that she'd once had under control. She couldn't believe she had been so close to cutting him, which could have meant her going to jail.

Valerie watched over Nicole in the bedroom. Keisha sprawled across the sofa, engaged in another gossip rag, but her mind was preoccupied with Tisha. Freda had dozed off. Zenora confessed to Renee that she wished she had warned the others earlier about the marks on Tisha's neck and that maybe she should not have had the stripper come like Denise said. Maybe, maybe, maybe.

"We didn't know Roland would burst in like that," Renee said to comfort Zenora. "And the stripper was really fun. I know I enjoyed him—even though he was black. The fault is not with you. Tisha is the one who put herself in that predicament, not us. But did you see how much she enjoyed herself while she was here? This was probably the best fun she has had since she married him."

Zenora felt somewhat relieved by Renee's words, but she was still upset by the happenings of the evening. One thing was for sure: She was not in the mood to meet Ernesto later.

Mira returned to the living room, trying to fan away any evidence of her smoking, and roused Freda from her light nap.

Denise checked her voice mail. She had nine messages, and the first was from Domenick, assuring her that the campaign-office fiasco was being addressed and that painters would be there the first thing Monday morning with mint green paint.

"That's a relief," she said aloud. She listened to her other messages, and one from her campaign manager caused her to call out to the other girls.

"You guys aren't going to believe this! My campaign manager left a message that the Philadelphia chapter of 100 Black Men will be sending a campaign check for twenty-five thousand dollars."

"Are you serious? That's great!" Zenora said.

"Yes, that is fantastic! I was getting a little concerned about contributions. The checks were coming in, but the amounts were too low to cover my expenses."

Freda asked, "Mira, were you smoking again? I thought you stopped that nasty habit."

"I did stop, but after tonight, I needed something to calm my nerves, and I knew nobody over here had any weed. So I just walked up to Seven-Eleven and bought a pack of Salems. I just smoked one and threw the pack away. How's Nicky doing?"

Valerie came into the living room to inform the girls that Nicole was still sleeping.

"You know, I never did like his ass," Keisha said, and the others murmured in agreement. "I remember when Tisha started dating him. She turned him down a number of times, but he was persistent. Tisha's rule was to never go out with anyone who came to the office as a client. I don't know why she broke it."

Denise said, "That's right. She was assigned to his case when she was a social worker. He surely did pour on the charm, and then the next thing we hear, they're getting married and having a baby."

Renee added, "Then before we knew it, he had Tisha thinking that her whole world revolved around him. Everything just happened so quickly."

Mira said, "I've got a bad feeling. She's got to get out of there before it's too late. Isn't there anything we can do legally, Denise?"

"Not really, unless we actually see him hit her or she

asks us for help. If she doesn't want to press charges, there's nothing anybody can do."

Mira said scornfully, "That's just like the fuckin' law—waiting until shit happens before doing something about it. I say we wait for him one night after he gets off work and jump him!"

"You know I'm down with that," Freda concurred, and they slapped a high five in accordance.

Keisha warned, "Girl, this is not *Set It Off*, and shit, we'll get caught. I can't do the jail thing—I'm too cute."

Nervously pacing the floor as she thought of another solution, Mira said, "We really ain't got to do it, Keisha. I'll bring a U-Haul truckload of diesel dykes from my club to kick his ass. You know like those lumberjack bitches who be all like 'What, nigga, what?!' He won't know what hit him." Mira air-boxed as she relayed her plan to destroy Roland.

"Y'all know my granny is from the islands, right? She be sayin' in her dialect, 'Mira, Mira, you want me to fuck him up, do you? All we need is a piece of him clothes: old pair draws, sock, or anything I can have. I light a candle, put a picture of him in a box, and take it to the backyard and bury it. That nigga will lose his eyesight for three days, I tay ya. Or when him sleep—and you make sure that nigga sleep—have Tisha sprinkle a little Cajun cayenne pepper mixed with a pinch of garlic salt and white vinegar on his manhood garden downstairs, then lay a pigeon fedder in the bed with him. Now, Mira, make sure that a *pigeon* fedder. Cover him up and leave the room. He'll get deathly ill for seven days straight. He tink it a virus or a cold that him can shake. He'll get worse and worse, and every time he go to take a little dick piss, that shit will burn like acid.' "

Keisha said, "Shut up with all that mojo shit."

Mira, still talking in a West Indian accent, said, "I'm serious, Keisha, or better yet, put a little eyedrop in his coffee that will knock that nigga out for forty-five minutes."

"Jesus, Mira, I didn't know your grandmother was from the islands. What island?" Valerie asked.

"Coney Island in New York."

The loud chatter and laughter brought Nicole out of her room. She assured everyone that she was okay and couldn't believe her nap had lasted more than an hour.

"Denise, I'm sorry I spoiled the entire party for everyone."

"Don't be silly. Plus, there was no way you could have known that jackass Roland was going to show off like that."

"Has anyone talked to Tisha since?"

"Yes, I tried calling her and got her voice mail. She called my voice mail back and said everything is fine," Renee said.

"And what about Kimmy?"

"Oh, she's still at her grandmother's."

Zenora asked Nicole, "Are you sure you're okay? Should we call Alan?"

"God, no. He'll worry all night. I'm fine. I just got too excited, and what went on tonight caused me to forget to eat on time. C'mon, let's open my gifts."

They were like children at a party rather than bachelorettes as they clustered around Nicole on the sofa.

"Which one should I open first? They're all so beautiful and too pretty to unwrap," Nicole said.

"Girl, all the money I spent on that gift, you *better* open it," demanded Keisha.

Nicole closed her eyes and grabbed a gift from the pile. The box was from Mira and contained a beautiful Waterford crystal picture frame with a photograph of the girls taken at the engagement party. Of course, everyone oohed and aahed and wanted Mira to provide them with additional copies of the picture.

Next was a gold envelope wrapped in matching organdy ribbon from Keisha: a five-hundred-dollar gift certificate to Bloomingdale's, Nicole's favorite store. Nicole was ecstatic.

From Renee she received two first-class round-trip airline tickets to Barcelona, Spain. Nicole screamed, and Zenora said, "If Alan doesn't want to go, I'll gladly take his place on that trip."

"This must be from Zenora," Nicole said. "I recognized the fuchsia paper, the same color as your shop."

"Yeah, I just noticed that, too," Freda said. "Everything you got is that color. Reminds me of Puerto Rican purple. I bet you make them Ricans wear it to bed."

"Now you caught on." Zenora smiled.

Nicole opened the oversized gift bag, which contained Victoria's Secret lingerie and three complimentary visits for a full spa treatment at Z's shop. Freda tried to talk Nicole out of one of the passes, but it didn't work.

Valerie's gift was a burgundy leather-bound family Holy Bible embossed with Alan and Nicole's names.

"This is from Freda. God knows what could be in this," Nicole said about the next gift she picked up. She took a peek inside the gift bag and quickly slammed it shut. "I'm not showing this. I'm not."

That aroused everyone's curiosity, and they convinced Nicole to take whatever it was out of the bag. Reluctantly and embarrassed, she complied, pulling out a very realistic replica of a ten-inch penis.

Freda said, "Yeah, girl, that's for those lonely nights when Alan gets on your damn nerves. Raheem will take care of the job, and he don't ever talk back!"

When the entire piece was exposed, Nicole noticed a bracelet of blue-white diamonds wrapped around the base. Nicole was surprised by the ten-incher, but the diamond bracelet took the gift over the top.

Freda said, "Dicks and diamonds, they're a girl's best friends." Everyone laughed.

"First of all, let me thank you all for my beautiful gifts," Nicole said as she tried to keep her emotions in check. "In spite of everything that happened tonight, I am so happy. How many girls can say that? You know what I mean. I'm marrying the man of my dreams, my best friends from high school are my bridesmaids, I have a great job at the bank, a new home is being built from the ground up for me. I *am* truly blessed."

Mira lit some candles and dimmed the lights for a second time. She then passed out crystal glasses and the magnum of champagne she had brought for the festivities.

Keisha said, "I'm blessed, too. I ain't got no man right now, but that's cool. I own my own business, own a Lexus and an Explorer, my health is on point, I'm beautiful, and—"

"Okay, we get it, you're blessed," Zenora said.

"Naw, all kidding aside," Keisha said, "I've got eight amazing women to call friends. I tell you all everything about me. Y'all know stuff my own momma don't know."

All the bachelorettes raised their glasses to toast life, love, and friendship.

Renee took a sip of champagne before saying, "Uhmm, delish. But do we really tell each other everything? I mean, think about that. We all have mad love and respect for each other, but do we really tell each other *everything*?"

"Well, there's some shit that just ain't none of your business," Freda said.

Denise added, "There is always a secret or two that people wouldn't share with anyone, but that's a natural thing."

Renee said, "I'm sure there's one thing that would shock each of us if we knew of it."

"I'm not playing that game," Mira said, shaking her head. Freda asked, "Something to hide, Mira?"

"No, but I think that this is ground that should not be covered tonight," she responded.

"Okay, Miss DeVoe," Keisha challenged, "tell us a secret about you that we don't know."

After taking the floor for a few moments, Renee willed the courage to share. "Okay, when I was seventeen—" She stopped and then continued. "—I . . . tried it with a girl."

"Tell me more," Mira said as some of the friends gasped. Freda looked thoroughly disgusted by the revelation.

"How did you get yourself into a situation like that, Renee?" Nicole asked.

"It was over a guy in high school. Remember Darren Stokes on the swim team?"

Keisha said, "You mean the bowlegged guy with the big—"

Nicole cut her off immediately. "Keisha!"

"Feet, I was going to say *feet*."

Renee ignored Keisha and continued her story. "Well, if you remember, I was crazy over him. He wanted me to do it with a girl while he watched."

Mira jumped in. "Hold up. Clarification, here—why do men have no problem watching two women get it on with each other or him joining in? But if the woman wants him to watch a porn tape with two dudes, he barks at that, walks out, calling her a freak? It's still the same sex getting it on."

Keisha said, "They ain't all barking, and they ain't all walkin' out. That's the ultimate turn-on for a straight man—two women."

Renee explained, "It only went as far as light kissing, but nothing more than that because it hit me: My self-respect and pride were being tested. He told me that if I loved him and really wanted him the way I said I did, then I'd do anything that he asked. And then I thought about it. How dare you judge my feelings and love on some sick sex act that's getting you off? When I refused, he said to me, 'That's why brothas don't deal with no dark-ass sistahs like you all.' The white girl left me stranded and standing in the middle of the room. I was so lucky, because to my surprise, when I flew out of the room, there was a line of his black teammates waiting to join in. Darren was just the warm-up. He and his teammates didn't like their egos bruised, so they spread the word that I had a tryst with a white girl and the entire swim team. I withdrew from every club in school. It was like everybody was looking at me as the slut of the swim team."

Nicole said, "I remember there was some type of rumor about you, but we all dismissed it as a lie and thought some jealous classmate started it. Girl, we didn't take that seriously back then." She hugged Renee, who took a huge sip of champagne.

Renee teared up and said, "Okay, who's next?" scanning the room for a response.

Freda asked, "Next for what?"

"Revealing a secret," Renee said quietly.

Silence.

"Oh hell, I'll go next. I escorted in college," Keisha confessed.

"What!" they exclaimed.

"Yeah, I did it for a whole semester. My parents weren't speaking to me, because I decided I didn't want to be an educator like them. I wanted to own my own business. When I changed my major, they cut me off. A girl in my dorm turned me on to it."

"You didn't have to do that," Nicole said.

"I know. Nobody said there was sex involved. There was no sex with those men. They paid for my company, and that was it.

"And I don't need you judgin' me," Keisha declared. "We all didn't have a silver spoon in our mouths from the day of conception until now, like you, Nicky."

"That's not fair," Nicole said.

"Bitch, life ain't fair," Keisha said, her tongue loosed by all the champagne and beer she had imbibed that evening.

"Keisha! Don't you dare attack Nicole in that way!" Zenora yelled.

"Girl, you know you need to apologize. Nicole has always been a good friend to you," Denise said.

Keisha took her time before speaking. "I'm sorry. I don't know what got into me. It's my own fault. Guess I'm just trippin' because I never told anyone about that, and here I am blurting it out now to y'all."

They met halfway for a hug, and Nicole said, "It's okay—and besides, that was yesterday. You now own a very successful bed-and-breakfast with your brother. So I would say the whole decision worked out well. Wouldn't you? We've all done stupid shit when we were younger. Whatever you did then has made you stronger."

"Thanks, you always know how to turn lemons into lemonade."

Valerie said, "That's Nicky: mother hen. Just wait until you and Alan have kids. Not only will they be loved, but they'll be spoiled rotten, too."

Nicole became very quiet and started to clean up.

Valerie noticed the change in Nicole's demeanor. "What's wrong? Nicky?"

"It looks like none of you will be a godmother for our children," Nicole said, and sobbed uncontrollably. "Because I can't have children."

The other ladies were stunned. No one knew how to react to the sad news. They all thought Nicole would have been the best mother out of all of them.

"Perhaps you guys should have known about this, but I didn't know how to tell you. All my life you knew there were two things I wanted the most: to get married and have children."

Freda approached her cautiously. "Does Alan know?"

"Yes, he does, and you know one thing, he was so sweet about it. He told me that, of course, he was saddened, but nothing was more important to his life than me. We thought about adoption—which is still an option—but I'm a woman. I should still be able to have my own kids. It's not fair, it's just not fair."

Denise eased away to the other side of the room.

Zenora tried to comfort Nicole. "It's okay, Nicky. Things change. You never know what God has in store for you two. Miracles do happen."

"I know. It has a lot to do with being diabetic. If I do become pregnant, there could be major complications, and I can't do that to Alan."

Keisha noticed Denise had moved to the other side of the room and had turned her back to the other women. "Are you okay, Denise?"

After a long pause, Denise responded, "I had an abortion five months ago. It just wasn't the time to have a kid. Besides, I would have to put off the election and I'm not sure if I am mother material."

"Wait a minute," Freda said, jumping up. "You say you're pro-life in your campaign commercials, but then you go and have an abortion. You're talking out of both sides of your mouth. You're just like a typical politician."

Denise rebutted by saying, "I am pro-life. That was the best decision for me at the time. Do you think it was an easy one? You think I haven't felt guilty about it?"

Not ready to back down, Freda said, "Then why did you do it?"

Bitterly, Denise shouted, "Because I was raped. Are you happy now? I had an abortion because I was raped."

Nicole's own reaction turned from being appalled to remorseful. "Do you want to tell us what happened?" Nicole asked gently. Sad eyes were on Denise as she sat at the dining room table and her story began to unfold.

"I—I—I was working at my firm late one night, and before I knew it, everyone was gone except our maintenance guy, Jim. As he was leaving, he offered to walk me to my car, but I told him no and that I would be fine. I told him he should go home and that I would see him tomorrow. By the time I got down to the garage, the only car left on the lot was mine. I opened the trunk and put my briefcase in it.

"When I closed it, I felt a hand over my mouth and a knife at my neck. He never said anything. He didn't have to. I knew he meant business. Duct tape was wrapped across my eyes and mouth. I tried to fight, but then I sensed he was not alone. There were two of them. I remembered having the strangest thought as I lay on the ground. It felt so cold. Here I was being raped and possibly even killed after they were through, but all I could think about was how strange it was that it was so hot in the garage that evening, yet the ground felt so cold against my body. When they were done, I just lay there very quietly. I wanted them to think I had blacked out.

"They never uttered a word to me or each other. They just buckled their pants and walked away like it was nothing. Sometimes I can still remember the smell of their cheap cologne and sweat. I remained silent and motionless even after I knew they were long gone. This may sound strange, but there was something comforting and secure about that cold ground. But I refused to prepare myself for death. Physically, I knew I needed to get up and leave, but mentally I felt safe being there alone where no one could see me.

"In reality, I knew that once I got up, I would have to deal with what had just occurred. When I did manage to get in my car, I went home. You know usually the first thing a rape victim does is take a shower. I didn't. I actually made myself a bite to eat and watched television before falling asleep on my sofa. When I woke up in the morning, I showered and went to the office like things were normal once again. Imagine that—worked all day, saw three clients, and went out to dinner with my campaign manager. That's me, still being in control. That's me—Denise always gotta be in control."

Denise collapsed. She started crying and shaking. "That's—that's me, Denise, always in control," she said again, her voice breaking.

Freda approached her and put her arm around Denise's shoulder. Nicole said, "You didn't have to bear this alone. You could have told me; you could have told any one of us."

"I know, but telling you about it would only cause me to relive the experience. Until this moment, I had filed it away and I never wanted to think about it again. Yes, I still get scared at night when I go to my car, but I refuse to change my habits because of what happened. I'm not going to let them defeat me," she said defiantly.

"You know that it wasn't your fault, right?" Zenora said. "What did the police say after you filed a report?" When Denise didn't answer, Zenora prodded, "You did file a report, didn't you?"

"No. What could the police have done? I never saw their faces. What description could I have given? I just wanted to get on with my life, and all I could think of was that I could have gotten AIDS. Becoming pregnant for some reason never entered my mind. How could I bring a child into this world not knowing who the father was? Why should my one night of hell become my child's lifetime of hell? Like I said, I had no choice."

Sighing heavily, Denise asked, "Could I get a hug?"

"Of course, girl," Nicole said, and they all moved to surround Denise for some sisterly bonding.

"Maybe I should have suggested another game!" Renee

said, hoping to break the tension. The women broke out in laughter, glad for the relief.

Mira pulled away from the hug. "Since we're telling secrets, I'll make mine short and sweet. I don't want to discuss it any further. I'm just going to say it because I haven't been completely honest with you guys tonight. Jeanette not being here with me tonight is not because she is upset about the water main break at the club. We've been separated for two weeks now. She's having second thoughts after all these years about our relationship. I couldn't believe it when she told me, and I blew the fuck up at her and we both said some things we shouldn't have. She moved out."

"But what about the club?" Renee asked.

Mira explained, "We're still partners, but we're just keeping it on the business tip right now."

"Things will work out, Mira," Nicole said. "Maybe Jeanette needs some time. Everyone knows how much that girl loves you."

Freda took her hand and said, "It's her loss, baby."

Mira was shocked. Freda was the last person she expected support from. "Thank you, Freda," Mira said.

It was now Freda's turn to open up. "Okay, I might as well get this shit—stuff—over with, and you guys have to promise me that you're not gonna laugh either."

Keisha and Zenora started laughing and guessed that her secret was probably something she has done sexually.

Freda said, "See what I mean?"

Keisha said, "Go 'head, girl, spill your guts."

Freda said, "Well, I really have been thinking about my life lately, spiritually, getting closer to God. Two months ago, I joined the church."

No one responded but Keisha. "What? A real church?"

Freda retorted, "No, bitch, a fake church! See even when I try to clean up my shit, people won't let me."

Renee asked, "What kind of church? Buddhism, Scientology, you know like Tom Cruise?"

Freda answered in anger, "Christianity, fool! Ain't no black people into Scientology. I'm becoming a Christian again."

Nicole said, "Visiting a church or joining a church isn't anything to be ashamed of."

"Oh, I'm not ashamed. I guess I am more worried about how I will be perceived in the recording industry. You know, will it hurt my career? The one thing I don't want is to turn off any record labels or producers. But you guys know me—I speak in the moment, I speak my mind, but this not-cussin' shit is hard."

"Well, just don't go to the opposite extreme and become a holy roller," Nicole cautioned.

"Well, I am proud of you, Freda," Valerie said. "Maybe religion is something that you've been lacking in your life."

"Bitch how you know what's lacking in somebody's life and you round here living like Condoleezza Rice," Keisha taunted. "You know she plays with 'bush.'"

Valerie ignored Keisha's vulgar remarks while Freda continued telling them of her life change and how reading the Bible and going to church had been difficult, but worth it all. "Haven't you noticed that I have not been cursing as much?"

"No," everyone said in unison.

"You know I think this is a good thing," Nicole said proudly as she looked at Freda. "Freda opened a topic that I want us all to talk about and I've been meaning to bring this up for some time now. To tell you the truth, I know that women say it as an endearment at times, but I don't like the fact that we routinely call each other 'bitches' all the time. And I'm not also feeling the word 'nigger' either. We need to stop."

Mira protested, "Why are you trippin', Nicky? I mean we all say it. Using the word *bitch* ain't always bad. There's a lot of different bitches, like, how many times have we said, 'I'm a bad bitch,' or 'She's a bitch,' or 'Bitch, please,' or my favorite, 'Bitch better have my money'?"

"Please, that's what I'm talking about, and we joke about it still. But we don't like it when 'other' people use the words *bitches* and *niggers*. We make it worse when we use it. Let's stop perpetuating this. I'm not a bitch, because I'm not a dog. And that's what a bitch is—a dog. That's also what slave masters called black female slaves. Bitches and bucks, that's what we were called. Too many of us forgot our history. Jews never forgot the Holocaust, so why do we have to forget slavery, and lynchings, and boycotts."

"Umm-hmm," the others agreed. A few moments passed in reflective silence.

After considering what Nicole said, Mira proposed,

"Okay, how about we make a pact right now not to use those two negative words anymore."

Everyone agreed except Keisha, who said, "Okay, I'll try. . . . I said I'll try, shit."

"Okay, I guess it's my turn," said Zenora. "It's not a bombshell or anything, but I'm starting my own wig line. It's still in the infant stages, and hopefully I'll be going international, so that means it will include Asian, Hispanic, and Caucasian selections."

"You better work, bi—, I mean, girl," Keisha said as she lifted up her hand for a high five.

All eyes turned to Valerie to see if she had anything to reveal, but she just shrugged her shoulders and said nothing.

Freda said, "Valerie ain't got no secrets. Y'all know she don't do nothin'." They all laughed until there was a knock at the door.

Fourteen

The Breakthrough

"I WONDER WHO that could be at this hour," said Freda. "Maybe it's Knight Rider comin' back to give us another ride!"

Freda answered the door to see Tisha standing in the doorway wearing sunglasses, a short jeans skirt, and a thin, wrinkled tank top. Her hair was messed up, and she clutched her large purse close to her chest. There was a deep cut in her bottom lip, and dried blood was encrusted around her nose. Her jaw was swollen, and there were prominent bruises around her neck. Her bare feet were bloody and grass-stained.

Tisha entered the apartment in a stupor. Everyone ran over to her. Renee reached for her shoulder, and Tisha winced in pain. Nicole led her over to the sofa, and the women started asking a barrage of questions.

Tisha was speechless and emotionless. Valerie reached for her sunglasses, but Tisha stopped her and removed them herself, slowly, revealing two very large black eyes as she lowered her head in shame.

"I really don't know when things changed. Roland went from being this caring, charming man who adored me to this abusive, controlling, and mean stranger. The first time he hit me, I literally was in shock. It surprised me so much that I didn't even feel the pain. Isn't that strange? Not feeling pain when it hurts so bad that you become numb. It was like my thoughts had not caught up with the reality of what had just happened. Only after tasting the saltiness of blood in my mouth did I realize I had been hit. It shocked him, too, because right after he did it, he began apologizing, crying, telling me how he didn't mean to do it and that if I would just do what he said, it wouldn't happen again.

"Why do we believe any of this when we know it's a lie? Sometimes he didn't hit me but I wish that he had. After being called a whore, a bitch, and a worthless piece of shit so many times, I actually welcomed his blows to my body because they were fast and over quickly. The name-calling seemed to linger in my head and heart much longer.

"It's easy for a bruised arm to heal. You just hide it and give it a few days. It eventually fades away, but how do you heal a broken heart? Sometimes after he beat me and fell off to sleep, I laid there beside him, petrified because I couldn't tell which sound was louder or more dangerous, the beating of my heart pounding through my chest or the sound of his voice booming over me. Over and over and over." Tisha drifted off for a moment and mumbled incoherent sounds, but no one wanted to interrupt her.

"I should have known better, but forgive me for not thinking too clearly. After being struck in the head and face so many times, the abuse paralyzed my mind and left me numb. Roland has this look—I can't describe it—it's like a glare when he grabs my face, and I knew what was coming next. For some reason, tonight it didn't matter how much he hit, slapped, kicked me, or called me names, I was finally leaving. He laughed at me. *Laughed at me!* Said leaving was not even an option because he would find me and kill me. If not, then he'd go after my family. All of you here are my family, and I was putting your lives in danger.

"Then out of nowhere he said, 'Go, bitch, but Kimmy stays here with me.' And then he raped me—he raped me like some wild animal, cursing that he would see me dead first before any other man would have me. I felt his anger as he tore into me then rolled me over before he went to sleep.

"That was the last straw. There would be no more forcing me to have sex, hitting, and talking down to me. I was tired. You ever just want to lie down and get some rest? Lie down and get some fuckin' rest?"

The women were silent as Tisha shared her story.

"I got up and went to the hall closet. It seemed like that was the longest walk of my life. I know he kept a loaded gun on the top shelf. See." Tisha pulled out a Smith & Wesson .44 and got up and erratically started pacing with it. The women froze in their tracks. Tisha flashed back to a vision of Roland sitting next to her and pointed the gun into Renee's chest. Renee was still in shock as the other women scattered for cover.

"There was only one way for me and my baby to be free. Don't you see? I checked the barrel to make sure there were bullets in the gun. If I didn't do it now, I wouldn't be able to do it ever again. Thank God, Kimmy wasn't home. I was not going to let him take her. Not take my baby. Not raise her to have an evil heart like him. As he laid on his back snoring, I stood over him by the bed and pointed the gun right at his heart. I wanted to destroy it; it was evil and rotten. If I shot it out of him, then I would be free.

"Roland heard a click and opened his eyes. I was releasing the safety device on the revolver. His eyes opened suddenly and startled me. I'm sure he saw the fear on my face. Laughing at me, he said, 'Put my shit back where you found it and take yo' ass to bed. I'll deal with you in the morning. Looks like my lesson tonight didn't get through to you. Stupid bitch.'

"I was so scared and just about ready to obey when he threatened me with those chilling words: 'You are such a dumb bitch, and if I don't get my daughter away from you, she will be a dumb bitch, too, then her husband will have to knock her on her ass and straighten her out like I did you.'

"I pulled the damn trigger!

"His last look seemed to say that he couldn't believe a 'dumb bitch' could do anything like that. I fired again.

Bang! To make sure that evil heart would pump no more. Blood was gushing out of his chest—evil blood. Blood was everywhere—on the bed, the floor, the wall, everywhere. *Bang,* again. This time I shot him right in his damn mouth that spoke all of those nasty words to me. *Bang.* Another shot right between his thighs, blowing his penis in half. His body jerked from the close impact of the bullet. The bastard bled like a pig, and one of his testicles spun to the other side of the bed. *Bang,* I shot again, and this time his face was blown into pieces. Where those hateful eyes once sat were now deep dark bloody holes. When he went to hell, nobody would recognize him.

"My bullet opened him up like a head of red cabbage— just like the vegetable he made me. The bastard—evil, dirty bastard. On the side of the bed was a picture of Kimmy splattered in blood. I couldn't leave her that way. The phone rang, and I stopped shooting. That's when I went into the bathroom and wiped the blood from her pretty image, and I cleaned off all that evil blood from my naked body. Just wiped and wiped and wiped. I'm safe here now with all of you."

Tisha seemed to go off into her own delirious world and began to mumble again incoherently. "There's no more voices in my head, Nicky, no more. He can't hurt me. This case is closed.

"Is the door locked? Is it locked? Here, let me clean up from the party. I'm not bad, I'll let you clean up. Who checked the door? Please check the door. Kimmy? Kimmy's safe, yeah, Kimmy is okay, she's safe. I got to go. I got to put starch in Roland's shirts. I got to go, he needs them for work, extra starch, extra starch. I'm not dumb, I'm not a whore. Just let me get him ready for work."

Nicole carefully approached Tisha and said, "Give me the gun, Tish. C'mon, baby, it's going to be okay. You're here now. It's safe. Just give me the gun." Nicole could see splattered blood on the barrel.

Tisha was like a scared rabbit and told Nicole, "I need it," as she held it to her chest.

"No, Tish, just let me have it, and we'll take care of you." The women were in various states of disbelief, shock, and fear.

Denise tried another way to get the revolver. "Tish, I need you to give me a dollar. Just give me a dollar."

Tisha didn't let go of that gun, but was able to pull a dollar bill out of her purse, and in a childish manner she turned over a crumpled dollar bill to Denise.

Keisha frantically asked, "What's the dollar for?"

"It will signify that Tisha has retained my services as her attorney."

"Attorney? Tisha does not need an attorney. It was self-defense. We know what he's done to her."

"The first thing we gotta do is call the police," said Keisha.

"No the fuck we don't," spat Mira. "I'm glad his ass is dead; it's long overdue. I say we go over there and get rid of the body."

"Are you serious?" Denise asked. "Do you know what we're dealing with here? Murder, murder!"

Nicole pleaded, "Let's think this through. Let's just think this through."

Tisha stoically stood up and turned to face the door. "It's okay. No need to worry. Everything will be fine, will be fine, but thank you so much for being my friends, my sisters, whom I love so much. I see how all of you light up when Kimmy is in the room, and that makes me feel so good, knowing that she has all these wonderful godmothers. Mira, can I have a cigarette?"

Mira looked for the okay to give her a Salem. Nicole nodded affirmatively, and Mira pulled out one of the smokes she said she had thrown away. She wanted to smoke it outside.

Denise said, "I need to drive you to the police station as your attorney and your friend."

"No, Denise. The press will be all over you," Freda said. "I'll go. With your election coming up, you don't need this kind of publicity."

"I don't care about that! Tisha is the most important person to me right now. I'm going to the police station with you."

Tisha shook her head.

Mira said, "There isn't any way we are going to let you leave here alone. Now, Denise goes with you, or we'll all go. It's your choice."

Tisha calmly said, "Okay, okay. Oh, Nicky, I never got a chance to give you my gift." She reached into the purse to hand her an envelope. "Promise me you won't open this until I'm gone."

Nicole nodded affirmatively and reluctantly reached for the sealed thin envelope as Tisha slowly released it from her grip. Nicole sensed that whatever was in the envelope had to be significant because she felt how difficult it was for Tisha to release it.

As Tisha painfully passed the envelope over to Nicole, she gave a deep sigh as if she were releasing all of her pain.

"Okay, you win, Denise," Tisha said with a weary smile. "I'll wait outside. I need to call Granny, who is watching Kimmy, to let her know where I'll be."

Nicole tried to keep her in the apartment as long as she could. "You can use the phone in my room if you need privacy, baby."

"I'm feeling light-headed and could really use some fresh air," Tisha said.

Keisha and Freda were silent souls timidly positioned behind the bar and ready to take cover if Tisha wanted to use that .44 again. The biggest horns suddenly had no engines.

Denise and Tisha were ready to leave and walked to the door.

Valerie asked, "Denise, can't we all go?"

Denise assured them that going along would only have them sitting around. "The police will only give me time with her because I'm her attorney."

Freda finally found her voice again. "Oh my God, Tisha is going to be charged with murder."

Mira silenced her. "Will you shut up?" Then she lit a cigarette, forgetting where she was, then quickly put it out and said, "Sorry, Nicky."

Denise and Tisha left. While the other women tried to recover from the shock of what happened to their friend, after a few moments there was a frantic ringing of the doorbell and banging on the door. "Open the door, open the door!" Denise shouted.

Meanwhile, Tisha impatiently waited for the elevator after pressing the down button again and again. She noticed a blinking light above the stairwell door. EXIT. It needed a new bulb, but the flashing attracted her to it. Those glaring red lights drew her closer and closer. Still clutching her purse, Tisha moved away from the elevator doors and followed that blinking red light to the stairwell. EXIT. EXIT. EXIT.

Nicole opened the door, and Denise quickly brushed by her, saying, "I forgot my keys. Where did I put my keys?"

"Denise, where's Tish?"

"She's at the elevator. Oh yeah, I was on the patio, right."

"Nicky, the gun," whispered Renee.

They all rushed toward the apartment door while Denise rushed to pick up her keys. "Shit, my keys."

"Tish, Tish." Everyone seemed to be calling her at once.

A loud boom pierced the air.

EPILOGUE

A New Day

NICOLE PAUSED in the church foyer. As she waited for Alan to join her, she looked at her friends in the sanctuary cooing over Kimmy. One year had passed since that dreadful night. Nicole had postponed her wedding for a month out of respect for Tisha, which gave everyone some time to heal and regain some normalcy in their lives.

All the friends were still very close and loving, and even though they didn't telephone or visit one another as much as they had in the past, each one knew that a friend was never farther than a phone call or letter away. They still disagreed, fought, and argued about the simplest of things, but Nicole could not imagine going down this journey of life without these women being a part of it.

Nicole thought back to her wedding day. When Freda

began to sing "All In Love Is Fair," that day déjà vu hit her, and Nicole realized that this was the dream she'd had the night before her bachelorette party. All her bridesmaids were lined up next to Reverend Roberts, just like in her dream, complete with Keisha holding Kimmy. In the dream, Tisha sat on the pew alone, but now Nicole felt that maybe Tisha hadn't been late after all and that it was Tisha's way of letting her know that whatever happened, she would be always there with her. Peace flooded through Nicole's body, and a smile came to her face.

Kimmy had adjusted well to Nicole and Alan. In fact, she ran the house and Alan, who adored her. Even though Kimmy was too young to remember her mother, Nicole vowed to keep Tisha's memory alive. Nicole felt that Kimmy needed and deserved as much attention as possible and suggested to Alan that she leave her position at the bank and become a stay-at-home mom. Alan couldn't agree more.

The first year was the hardest because every time Nicole looked at Kimmy and held her, she started crying. Kimmy was so energetic and sweet, and no one could look at her and not see Tisha. As happy as Nicole was to have Kimmy, there was still some sadness, and she still wasn't sure what she would tell Kimmy, when she was old enough, about her mother. However, it would be the truth. Tisha's grand-mother, Kimmy's only blood family, was in a convalescent home, but Nicole made sure she saw as much of Kimmy as possible.

Roland's sister, Grace, overdosed and was found dead

on the steps of the Broad and Susquehanna subway station. She weighed a mere eighty-five pounds and was discovered wearing tattered and dirty clothing. The only possessions she had when her body was found were a crack pipe and a wallet-sized torn picture of her niece, which was inscribed, "To my Aunt Grace from Kimmy, one year old."

As Denise reached for Kimmy, Nicole couldn't help but notice how happy she looked. Denise ultimately lost the city council election, but now she headed the largest black law firm in the city. Denise hadn't given up on politics and, as a matter of fact, was planning her strategy for the 2010 election. The previous election had increased her profile in the city, and as Denise had said, first she'd be elected in Philadelphia and then she'd run for a national office. But she had something else to take into account when planning out her career goals: She'd been seeing Domenick, the painting contractor. They started getting more acquainted after the campaign-office mishap. Work and career were still her priority, but after revealing her secret at the bachelorette party, Denise said the pain was almost completely gone. Once a week Denise volunteered her services at a rape crisis center.

○ ○ ○

DENISE PASSED KIMMY to Freda, who was there briefly from Europe. The tour with Freda Payne proved to be the best thing that could have happened to Freda's career. Two European record producers were looking for a sexy singing "black chick" for the release of a hot new dance record, and Freda was offered a deal. The record was titled, *Movin' On*, and that was exactly what Freda's career was doing as it topped the European dance charts. Freda's solo performances were in demand all over Europe, and the record was just now making a little noise in the States.

And, Freda was also in love; she'd nabbed herself an Italian. Sergio was a restaurateur who became smitten with Freda after seeing her at a club in Paris. The last time she and Nicole had spoken, Freda was learning Italian. She told Nicole that spiritually, she was on solid ground—her cursing had stopped and she was not so judgmental. Before Freda had left for Europe, Nicole had talked with her about her bitterness about her life and career and had given her a copy of *The Secret* DVD and encouraged her to take heed. Nicole wasn't sure if that had anything to do with Freda's transformation, but she was happy for her friend nevertheless.

Nicole watched Zenora lean in and make a kissy face at Kimmy. Zenora had tried to focus on the business end of her salon, but that was short-lived. She missed the compliments from her personal clients and the joy of styling hair. She kept her word and opened a third salon with Rocky as her partner called Z-Roc's, which was located in the up-scale Liberty Place Mall in downtown Philadelphia. Her wig and weave line, Zenora with a Z, was flourishing, and good word of mouth as well as ads in *Essence, Ebony,* and *Upscale* magazines drew the customers in. She has been dating someone seriously—Rocky's brother, José. She said she was "keeping it all in the family!"

Her no-nonsense approach to lateness was still intact. A couple of months ago, Nicole got stopped by police on the way to her salon because of a wrong turn. Needless to say, she was late for her appointment, and when she arrived at the shop, Z said, "Girl, I feel you—I really do, but I just can't reach you! Reschedule." Nicole was pissed at first, but it didn't matter—she had to reschedule. By the time she got to her car, she actually started laughing about it.

Kimmy reached over and grabbed Renee's hair. The long blond weave that never really fit her had been replaced with a shoulder-length honey-brown style that made her look softer. The contacts had also been thrown away. Unfortunately, Renee's soap opera, *Tomorrow Will Come,* was canceled earlier that year after a four-year run, but she did gain one thing from the soap—a boyfriend. She's been dating Jackson Weldon, the "block" man she at first despised, who was now playing the lead role in a Broadway version of *Lilies of the Field,* based on the old Sidney Poitier film. She has been contemplating a move to L.A. at the urging of her agent, Josh, who felt he could do more for her through the L.A. office. She was recently cast as the lead role in a film by a new filmmaker, Fred Thomas, Jr., out of Philadelphia called *Sorors,* which had been getting a lot of buzz and attention on the festival circuit.

Nicole saw Mira reach over to tickle Kimmy. She and Jeanette didn't get back together, and they'd sold the Loose Balloon. Jeanette was living a straight life. Mira was still in love with Jeanette, and for a while when she talked about her, Mira said this was just a phase that Jeanette was going through and that she knew she'd be back. However, when she found out that Jeanette was pregnant, she sort of shut down for a while.

But things were looking up for her: Mira took her proceeds from the sale of the club and opened a little trendy coffeehouse in Manhattan's Chelsea neighborhood. She was also dating again. She and Catherine, an older white woman, lived together, but Mira made sure the only name on the coffeehouse was that of Mira Ranks.

Wanting some time with her goddaughter, Keisha playfully grabbed Kimmy from Mira's arms. After her brother, Kevin's, scandal, Keisha stopped speaking to him for about six months. She felt that he'd embarrassed her and their parents. She had known he was promiscuous and had always warned him to be careful, but this scandal took it to another level. Because of his public popularity, he dominated the rag sheets. Local news stations continuously ran the scandalous items nightly on the news, as well as getting mentioned on the national news and syndicated shows like *Entertainment Tonight, Access Hollywood,* and *TMZ.*

In fact, his own station ran various stories—all for ratings. A lot of what they said were lies—but most were the truth. Kevin had had no idea that Dahlia was a transsexual. Keisha found herself defending her brother daily because of the lies and misconceptions. Keisha no longer supported the tabloids. Whenever she was questioned about her brother or the scandal, her reply was, "Fuck y'all, and mind yo' own damn business!" Keisha was still Keisha: loud, brazen, bold, and crazy.

At first Nicole was a little angry with her because she thought that it was time that Keisha grew up and changed her ways. But then Nicole realized that she couldn't change her friends. They were who they were, and for whatever reason, she'd chosen them as her friends. They should accept themselves for who they were, as long as none of them were intentionally being hurtful.

Nicole had to admit, at the end of the day, none of them really wanted Keisha to change, because it was her craziness that they all loved about her. Keisha said and did things that most only thought about but wouldn't dare say or do. You had to respect someone like that. Whenever anyone was down and needed a pick-me-up, Keisha could be counted on to keep it real—maybe a little too real. People knew immediately where they stood with her, and that was what people respected. She still loved the clubs and partying but was always one of the first ones there if any of her friends needed her.

Valerie put her arm around Keisha as she leaned in to kiss Kimmy. She had closed on the building, and her day-care center was thriving. Valerie's life was simple and carefree. She said that marriage and children would be nice, but she was not worried about it if it didn't happen. Keisha still would tease her and say she was becoming an "old settler." But Valerie knew that she was content and loved her drama-free life. Men of all colors and status asked her out, but she warned them at the door that there would be no sex. It wasn't a religious decision, just a personal one, and she didn't care if others didn't get it. At Nicole's bachelorette party, Valerie never got a chance to reveal her secret or say if she had one. What was Valerie's secret? *Did* she have one? She insisted she didn't, and everyone believed she was telling the truth.

Nicole rubbed her stomach. Five months ago, she discovered she was pregnant. The doctors had been monitoring her very closely, and although they had advised her *not* to get pregnant, Nicole knew it was God's will. Alan constantly called her during the day to check up on her.

Nicole felt that God had blessed her. In her heart, she knew that their baby would be fine. She and Alan found out that they were having a girl. When she asked Alan what they should name her, he said, "Why not Adrienne?" Alan's suggestion brought tears to Nicole's eyes. How could she help loving this caring, sensitive man.

When Nicole announced her pregnancy, Denise immediately told her that she would be planning the biggest baby shower ever! Nicole smiled at the memory. *Gotta love Denise. At least she's consistent.*

Nicole looked toward the pew where Tisha had sat in her dream and thought about something her nana had once told her: "You know, baby, some people are not meant to go the distance with you. They are only on the train of your life until their stop comes up. And then they got to get off, baby. Some are here for a season and a reason, and fewer for a lifetime, 'cuz dat's the way it's s'pose to be."

ACKNOWLEDGMENTS

There are so many people to thank that it could actually be another novel, but I want to first give thanks to God for blessing my life! My brother, Vernon, who is so proud of his big brother. My editor, Melody Guy, who found me in cyberspace and believed in me since our first phone conversation. To the One World/Ballantine staffers: "Thank you for everything!"

Much love to Ruth Blake, Beck Davis, Zeus Benitez, Delores Wilson, Esq.—my attorney and friend for seventeen years. "Has it really been that long?" The Manley family, Rodrick Paulk, Phillip Fields, Michael Tyler, the Garcias, all my kids, Tamika Patton, Vivian Harmon, Will Smith, Sr., the Smith Family, Shoneji Loraine.

To Fred Thomas, Jr., and Chris M. Dabney, my friends and business partners, the entire cast of *The Bachelorette*

Party stage play, and to every actor ever cast in a Don B. Welch production. Dawnn Lewis, Vanessa Bell Calloway, Ananda Lewis, Callie Rogers, Sharon O. Walker, and Freda Payne—my sisters for life. Evan Reynolds, Betty Spivey, Judy Pace, Tatyana Ali, Lynn Hamilton, Hill Harper, Loretta Devine, LaWanda Page, Mary White, Catarah Hampshire, Steven Gibbs, Wade Redcross, Jason Overstreet, José Alvarado, N. D. Brown, Brenda Vivian, Dorien Wilson, "Terezen," "Leola," Scherrie Payne, Kevin King, Jana Babatunde-Bey, Dwayne Dantzler, Alex Velasquez, Dominick Reyes, Anna Maria Horsford, Patti LaBelle, Jefferey Turner, DeVida Jenkins, Gayle Samuels, Bill Golden, Charles T., Teddy R., Dez Coleman-Jackson.

To my Maryland and Philly extended families, Kenny and Chante Lattimore, Donn Swaby, Veronica Galvan, Cassi Davis, Steve M. To Ginuwine: "my talented new brother." Also love to Elisa P., Jarvis M., Juanita H., Mike Rivera, Orlando Berrios, Kenya Dean, Roland and Rose Dunston, "Nicky," "Mandy," "Brittney," "Ciara," "Jeff, Jr.," Steve Page, Marla Gibbs, Mary Wilson, Eleanor Jean Hendley, Latoya Pollitt, Tony Pollitt, Kyle Pollitt, Carolyn Pollitt, Louise Crawford, Mary White, Snap, Atif, Damon and Ramon, Ronald Young, Elisa T., Tanya Kersey, Fleace Weaver, Richard F., Sandra Kitt, Eddie Goines, Adam Wade, Alex Hamilton, Pam Jones, Steve Abram, Michael Letterlough, Jr., Contrella P. Henry, Danny A., Carol Roberts, Claudia Adams, Keith Burke, Kiyano Lavin, Allen Adams, Gail Silver, Anita Davenport, Pastor(s) Barry and Kimberly Lyons, Kenyon Glover, Paul Jerome, Terell Daluz,

Rylan Williams, "Anju," Claudia Adams, Joahn Webb, Donna Gibbs-Jones, Lisa Thompson, Jay Jones, Raufel, Charmaine, "Hatch," and all the girls of the *BP* stage play: Kiki, Shoneji, Raquel, Caryn, Cerall, Khalilah, Audrey, Emayatsy, Tiffany, Nicole, Brenda, Janora, Milauna, Tanjereen, Annette, Mylika, Paulette, Roman, Sabah, and Keena. To Professor Sandra Johnson—thank you for everything you've done for me with this book and for many years of friendship. Thank you all for touching my life!

To those who I forgot, I'll get you in the second novel.